continued . . .

"A delectable treat for cozy lovers, British style."
—*Kirkus Reviews*

"A delight . . . warm, vivid descriptions."
—*Time Out* (London)

"The fundamental British cozy . . . first-class."
—*Midwest Book Review*

Also by Hazel Holt

MRS. MALORY AND AND DEATH IS A WORD

A Sheila Malory Mystery

Hazel Holt

AN OBSIDIAN MYSTERY

OBSIDIAN
Published by New American Library,
an imprint of Penguin Random House LLC
375 Hudson Street, New York, New York 10014

This book is a publication of New American Library.

First Obsidian Printing, May 2015

Copyright © Hazel Holt, 2014

For more information about Penguin Random House, visit penguin.com.

ISBN 978-1-101-99063-6

Printed in the United States of America
10 9 8 7 6 5 4 3 2 1

Penguin
Random
House

For all my readers, past and present,
with love and gratitude

Death is a word
Not to be declined in any case.

Chapter One

"So how was Eva?"

"Upset, of course," Rosemary said, "but you know how she is, always cheerful and positive about things."

"It was so *unfair*," I continued, "just six months after he'd finally retired . . ."

Eva's husband, Alan Jackson, was a foreign correspondent, a familiar face on our television screens in exotic places, all too often with burning buildings and shellfire lighting up the darkness behind him.

"Of course he should have retired years ago," Rosemary continued, "but there was always just one more job. Still, after all that Middle East stuff he promised Eva he'd call it a day."

"I really don't know how she's been able to live with it all these years."

"Well, she knew when she married him that's how

it would be. Goodness knows, the family tried to persuade her not to, but she always said she'd rather have that sort of life with Alan than a settled one with anybody else. She could have married Gerald—he was mad about her—and ended up as a judge's wife, *Lady* Forsyth!"

Eva Jackson is Rosemary's cousin ("umpteen times removed") and she's always been very fond of her. Indeed we all are. It's difficult to describe her—lively, amusing, down to earth, clever without seeming clever, sympathetic, a good listener—I could go on. She's simply Eva, a large woman in every sense. "I really ought to diet," she says ruefully, "but I never seem to have the time." Which is true. When she moved back to Taviscombe after Alan's death, she was eagerly pounced on by the local charities always on the lookout for energetic volunteers. When we protested she said, "It does me good to keep busy."

It's ironic that Alan, who had survived so many hazardous experiences—under cross fire in the Balkans, yomping with the marines in the Falklands, dodging snipers in Libya and interviewing Taliban warlords in the back of a Toyota truck, madly driving through the dust in Afghanistan—should have died in a London hospital of kidney failure. Eva had watched all these perils with a sort of stoicism.

"I suppose," I said, "she understood all the dangers, being a journalist herself."

"Being a feature writer on a Sunday paper," Rosemary replied, "isn't quite the same thing."

"Well she has done some investigative stuff."

"Checking on pharmaceutical companies and care homes isn't really in the same league."

"I suppose not."

"Anyway," Rosemary said, "she's still got a garage full of boxes so I said I'd go round and help her sort them out. Mostly books and papers—she just unpacked the practical things she needed and left all the other stuff. A lot of it's Alan's and I don't think she could face it right away."

"Easier with the two of you."

"Well, at least I can help her heave the boxes about."

When I saw Rosemary a day or two later, I asked how it had gone.

"We did a bit, but it's a mammoth task! Lots of Eva's old articles, notes Alan made, maps and reports—masses of correspondence—I don't believe either of them ever threw anything away. And hundreds of books. She's going to need yards and yards of bookshelves."

"I'll give Dave a ring, if you like—he did a lot of carpentry for Michael and Thea when they first moved into their house."

"Good idea. Actually, I thought she needed a bit of a break so I asked her to lunch tomorrow and I hope you'll come too."

"Fine. I'd love to see Eva again, but I didn't like to call or anything when she's only just moved in."

"The friends down here from way back have all moved away, so I thought you and I might rally round."

Eva's parents lived just outside Taviscombe and she was brought up here. Her father was an Australian, but his family originally came from Somerset. Apparently her grandfather quarreled with *his* father way back, when he didn't join up in the First World War because he was a pacifist. He (the young man) went to Australia, married there and, dramatically, never mentioned his family again, but his son, Eva's father, did volunteer in 1945 and came to England to join the RAF. After the war, he came down to Exmoor to have a look at the place his family came from and decided that this was where he wanted to live. He married a local girl (from quite a well-off family) and, with their help, set up a small engineering factory which did very well and eventually made him a rich man in his own right. It always seemed to us a very romantic story and, as girls, we envied Eva for having such an unusual family.

Eva was some years younger than Rosemary and me, but we took to her straightaway. Rosemary, whose mothering instincts were very strong even then, took Eva under her wing and, even now, is very protective of her.

Eva went to boarding school but spent her holidays at home, so Rosemary and I saw quite a bit of her when she was young. But, after Oxford, like so many of that generation, she was mad keen to go to London—where it was "all happening"—and we saw her only infrequently, when she visited her parents or sometimes when we stayed with her in her chaotic flat in Bloomsbury near the British Museum, when we felt like a trip to London.

It had been quite a while since I'd seen Eva. Rosemary and I had gone up to London for the funeral—a formal affair at St. Bride's off Fleet Street, with some well-known faces, broadcasters, politicians, other journalists—but, of course, it hadn't been possible then to do more than murmur a few obvious words of sympathy.

She was already there when I arrived, a glass of red wine in her hand, and Rosemary's old boxer dog asleep with his head resting heavily on her feet. She waved her glass in greeting.

"Sorry I can't get up," she said smiling, "but Alpha here has got me pinned down. No," she went on, as Rosemary made a move to remove him, "I like him there—it's very comfortable."

I went over and gave her a hug. "Lovely to see you. How are you finding the cottage?"

"Cozy, I think the word is. I thought it would be easier to manage after that large flat, but I do miss the space—there's nowhere to put things. And, because I'm hopeless at packing I left it all to the removal men and, bless them, I'm sure they did a good job but they've packed *everything*, even some old pencils and rubber bands! I suppose it's like computers—you give them an instruction and they take it literally!"

"Oh dear. Rosemary tells me you need more bookshelves. I can recommend a good carpenter."

"That would be marvelous—that is, if he can find enough wall space. Another thing I've discovered about an eighteenth-century cottage is that none of the walls are straight—they sort of *curve*, if you know what I mean."

"Only too well. No, Dave is quite used to that— he's very good. I'll give you his number."

"I suppose I ought to do a bit more sorting out. I really haven't any idea what I want to keep. As I said, they obviously emptied all the bookshelves and filing cabinets into boxes. It's all a bit daunting. Rosemary's been an angel and got me going—I'd really like to leave them there, *in situ*, and try and forget they ever existed. But it wouldn't be fair to leave it all to Dan after I've gone."

Dan is Eva's son, their only child, also a journalist, though also in another field; he's a restaurant critic, well known for his acerbic comments on the page and on many television programs.

"How is Dan?" I asked. "I loved his piece about that new place in Notting Hill—do they really serve the food on pieces of slate? It's bad enough that practically everywhere you go the food comes in enormous soup plates!

Eva laughed. "Oh, he's off to do some sort of gastronomic tour of Spain. I think it's for that food program. I can't keep up with him."

"Well," Rosemary said, "I'm glad he's not here to comment on my little offering. Come along both of you, and bring your glasses—lunch is ready."

The next time I saw Eva was at Brunswick Lodge, the cultural center of Taviscombe as my friend Anthea, who runs the place, likes to describe it.

"Oh, any subject at all—I'm sure whatever you choose will be fascinating," Anthea was saying.

"Well, I'd love to, of course, but I do seem to have taken on rather a lot already . . ."

"Oh, it doesn't have to be anything *formal*, just a little chat, really, and I'm sure people would like to ask a few questions. After all," she continued, "we don't often have the chance to hear about the life of a famous foreign correspondent, quite a *celebrity*. About an hour would be fine, a bit longer if there's a lot of questions and, of course, if we could manage some sort of film—"

"Sorry to interrupt, Anthea," I said, moving toward them, "but Rosemary needs to have a word with Eva. I think it's urgent."

With the benefit of years of experience, I managed to extract Eva from Anthea's clutches and take her into the kitchen where Rosemary was washing up after the coffee morning we had just been attending. She looked up inquiringly.

"I thought she needed rescuing," I said. "Anthea is a bit full-on at the best of times and she's really determined to pin down poor Eva."

"You'll have to do it in the end," Rosemary said, wringing out the dishcloth. "But you really don't need that now—especially," she said sternly, "with all that stuff in the garage."

"Perhaps I could help," I said. "An extra pair of hands."

"That would be marvelous," Eva said gratefully. "If you're sure you can spare the time. I know I've got to do it; I just need energizing."

"Right, then," Rosemary said briskly. "How about Wednesday?"

Eva's cottage, a few miles outside Taviscombe, is down a narrow lane with practically no passing places—you just pray you won't meet anyone. It stands alone, set back a fair way from the road and is not, by any means, a pretty cottage. Although the structure is built of the local red sandstone, the thatched roof has long since been replaced by more utilitarian slates, which, with its tiny windows, gives it a bleaker look. Originally it had been two small cottages, built for agricultural workers in the days when farming was more labor intensive than it is today. Even so, it's not very large and I could quite see what Eva meant about the lack of space.

"Not a single cupboard in the place," she said as she showed me round, "except for the space under the stairs and that's so dark you can't see what's in there."

Still, in spite of its unprepossessing exterior, the inside was unmistakably Eva's. The furniture seemed to have settled in comfortably and her possessions and the things that Alan had picked up in his travels gave it a familiar look.

"How about some coffee?" Eva asked.

"Coffee afterward," Rosemary said firmly. "I know you two—once you get settled there's no moving you."

Eva led us out through the back door into a large garden, now largely run wild.

"I really must get all this seen to," she said helplessly. "I simply don't *know* about gardens. We always lived in flats—not even a window box."

"Sheila will help you there," Rosemary said. "Her gardener likes a challenge."

Eva's garage wasn't a garage *per se*, being a large stone building a little way from the house with a frontage onto the lane.

"I think it must have been a woodshed or something," she said, fishing in her pocket for a key. "Oh, this wretched padlock—there, that's done it. I know I should keep it locked up but, honestly, I can't imagine anyone wanting to steal anything in here." She looked despairingly at the sealed boxes which filled the whole place. "There are times when I wish someone *would*."

"I think it was probably a cider house," I said, looking with interest at those bits of the walls I could see. "Too large for a woodshed. Still, being large is good—you'll be able to get your car in here all right, when we've moved all these."

"When!"

Rosemary, who had been examining some of the boxes near the door, opened one of them. "This lot seem to be books. I think we should concentrate on the books and leave the papers until later, then you can see how many new shelves you'll need. I'll just open up a few more of these, then we can take them into the house and sort them there."

We labored away for quite a while. It was a tiresome job—easier when Rosemary found an old wheelbarrow for carrying the boxes back to the house—unpacking the books in the little sitting room and then carrying them upstairs to the spare bedroom. After a while, Eva sat down firmly.

"Too late for coffee. I'm going to take you both out to lunch. No, Rosemary, dear, we've done enough for one day."

While we were washing the dust off our hands, Rosemary said to Eva, "If you'll give me the key I'll go and lock up the garage. I know you—you'll forget all about it and, although I know you'd like all that stuff to disappear, I don't believe in actually encouraging crime."

Eva pulled a face and fished the padlock key from her apron pocket. "I know you're right, Rosemary dear, but really, no one ever comes down the lane. Whose car shall we go in?"

After that, whenever we had time, Rosemary and I helped to move boxes.

"However many we do," I said, "it never seems to make any impression."

"I know," Eva said despairingly. "I think they multiply in the night."

But, eventually, most of the books were rescued and shelves put up to accommodate them—the few that Eva could bear to get rid of ("*Pastoralism in Tropical Africa*—no, I've never read it but it's one of Alan's; I must keep that. You can ditch the one on home economics, though—it was a review copy; I can't think why I kept it") were sent to various charity shops and only the papers, now housed in several filing cabinets, were left in the garage.

"No, I can't be bothered to sort them now," Eva said firmly. "And, no, I don't particularly want to put my car in there; it's perfectly all right in the lane."

Rosemary shrugged and said, "It seems a pity not to get the whole thing done properly. You know how it will be—you'll never get around to them now." Rosemary hates to leave any job half finished.

"As a matter of fact," Eva said, "I may have to do something about them. I had an e-mail from Geoffrey Bailey—you know, he was Alan's publisher."

Alan had written several books about his various assignments which had been very well received, though I remember Eva's descriptions of how difficult it was to get him pinned down in one place long enough to get anything written. "And, of course, who had to cope with the copy editor's queries and read the proofs?" she said. "Poor Geoffrey was tearing his hair out when he needed an answer urgently to some query and Alan was in a desert somewhere and the phone had broken down. Anyway, Geoffrey wants me to write a sort of short 'life,' as an introduction to Alan's unpublished stuff."

"That would be splendid," I said. "Is there much there?"

"God knows. As you saw, there's a mass of papers and I do rather dread tackling them, but now I have an actual reason for doing it, I really must get down to sorting them out."

"Will you edit them yourself?" I asked.

Eva shook her head. "I'm not sure. Geoffrey has a couple of people in mind who could do it, but . . ." She hesitated. "I suppose I feel I *should* do it—one last thing I could do for him."

She looked at me. "You'll understand, Sheila."

Although I've been a widow for many years now, I can remember how it was when Peter died and how I felt the need to pin him down, as it were, by doing something to affirm the fact that he had been a person, unique in his own right and not just a memory, fading with time.

"Yes," I said, "I understand. And I think it's a very good idea for you to have a special project. Anyway, if someone else did it they'd always be referring back to you—there'll be things only you know about, not to mention dates and so forth."

Eva groaned. "Not dates! I'm hopeless at dates— I barely know what day of the week it is."

Rosemary continued to lament the fact that Eva's garage was still full of unsorted papers.

"It really wouldn't take long just to get them organized in a general way—chronologically or something, and at least she'd know what was *there*."

I laughed. "She'll get around to it, eventually—Geoffrey will see to that. But you know how it is," I continued. "She's putting it off because she still hasn't really accepted that Alan won't be back to sort them himself. It does take a while."

"Yes, of course, I'm an idiot not to have realized. I shouldn't have pushed her to do all that clearing out."

"No, one needs a push, to be energized, as Eva said, otherwise it would be easy just to sit back and let things flow over you."

"Not Eva! She's so positive."

"Even Eva," I said sadly.

Chapter Two

Eva seemed to settle in quite well. She was busy with her committees, and, being a sociable person, made new friends. Rosemary and I saw her often and, since she no longer had relatives living here, I think she looked on Rosemary and me as her real family.

"She's taken on too much," Rosemary grumbled. "People take advantage of her good nature."

"They always have done," I said. "It's what she's used to. Anyway, she's got to fill her time with something."

"She could be working on the book. That would keep her occupied."

"She will, when she's ready. Not yet, though."

"No, I suppose it's a bit soon." She thought for a moment. "Why don't we all go to the theater in

Bath—there's always something good on there. Or the Old Vic at Bristol. I'm sure she must be missing the theater; she used to go all the time."

"You could ask her."

But Eva said she'd love to go sometime but she was a bit busy just at the moment and the most Rosemary could persuade her to was a visit to a garden center and a cream tea.

"Leave her alone for a bit," I said. "I expect she just wants to make a life for herself in Taviscombe. She knows we're here if she wants us."

"I suppose so," Rosemary said reluctantly. "It's silly to keep fussing. It's just that I want to help. After all, she is my cousin . . ."

After a while Eva had to go up to London. "To see Alan's solicitor," she said, "and I thought I might spend a little time with Dan; he's got a spare room in his flat. And there are lots of people I really ought to catch up with, while I'm there."

I wondered if Eva might have invented the need to go away, far away from the filing cabinets filled with papers, but Rosemary said, "I believe Alan left things in a bit of a muddle—not surprising given the way he was always traveling around. I think he intended to sort things out when he retired but, poor soul, he never got around to it. Eva's all right for money. She earned quite a bit when she was working and she still does the occasional article, but there's probably some legal stuff she has to do."

"Dan might help?" I suggested.

Rosemary laughed. "Oh he's the last person!"

"Oh?"

"*Not* exactly practical. Lives in a world of his own."

"But surely—the job, the TV?"

"Oh, that's Patrick. He's a sort of secretary, nanny, boyfriend, all in one. Dan relies on him for everything."

"Goodness, I never knew."

"It seems to work out all right and Eva is devoted to him, very grateful for all he does for Dan."

So Eva went off to London and Rosemary was able to stop fussing over her and concentrate on the demands of her mother, who was conducting a war of attrition with the local surgery concerning the alterations they proposed to make to her medication.

"She's convinced," Rosemary said, sighing heavily, "it's all about saving money and she's probably right, but Mother doesn't exactly *believe* in the Health Service as a national institution—she considers it exists solely for her personal benefit. It was all right when Dr. Macdonald was around—he was used to her—but, now he's retired, it's difficult. I try not to let her loose on them but you know how she is, and she's bitterly offended all the receptionists, even the nice sympathetic ones."

"Oh dear."

"I suppose I'll have to go and sort things out at the surgery and *then* try and explain it to Mother!"

* * *

With Christmas looming on the horizon, plans for various activities were already under way at Brunswick Lodge. This year it seemed that the usual Christmas Fayre was to be supplemented by an auction.

"An auction would be just the thing. We need to raise enough for a new carpet in the main room," Anthea said at the committee meeting. "The present one is wearing quite thin in places and I'm sure it constitutes a hazard."

"What sort of hazard?" Derek Forster demanded. Derek takes his position as treasurer very seriously and is engaged in perpetual conflict with Anthea over any expenditure, however small. Something major like a carpet gave him a splendid excuse to impede her in every possible way.

"It might go into a hole and someone might catch their foot in it. It's a health and safety issue," Anthea concluded grandly.

"Rubbish!"

"It's all very well to say rubbish," she countered, "but you wouldn't like to have to pay the compensation."

"We're covered by insurance, as I'm sure you know and, anyway, there *isn't* a hole, nor is there likely to be in the foreseeable future."

"Anyway," Anthea said, deftly changing tack, "it looks quite dreadful. It lets the whole place down.

I must remind you that, under our tenancy agreement with the council, we are *obliged* to maintain the Lodge in good decorative order."

"A carpet isn't decoration," Derek said with elaborate patience.

The whole business might have gone on indefinitely, as it often did, if Matthew Paisley hadn't interrupted to say he had to go because they had friends coming to dinner and he thought an auction was a good idea, whatever it was for, and should we put it to the vote. So we did and it was passed (only Derek opposing) and we all went home.

Anthea, of course, was in her element organizing the auction, Derek having officially washed his hands of the affair, though actually keeping a beady eye on the whole proceedings.

"Ah, Sheila, just the person," she said, unfairly trapping me when I had simply dropped in at Brunswick Lodge to leave a message about a booking for a meeting of the Archeological Society. "I want Michael to go in his Land Rover and pick up a bookcase and a small table from the Shelbys—they're expecting him on Saturday morning so if he can just give them a ring to let them know what time he'll be coming."

"I don't know if he's free on Saturday . . ." I began, but Anthea had already turned to greet someone.

"Sheila, this is Donald Webster," Anthea said, indicating a tall, good-looking middle-aged man. "He's recently moved to Taviscombe."

"I've just retired," he said. "I used to live in London . . ."

"Donald is going to be very useful," Anthea said enthusiastically. "He's agreed to take the auction for us. Isn't that splendid?"

Her victim gave me a slight smile but said nothing.

"Such a good way to join in things," Anthea said, "get to know people."

She moved away to interrupt a conversation between Matthew Paisley and another of the helpers.

"Did you actually volunteer to do the auction?" I asked.

Donald Webster laughed. "Not in the strict sense of the word," he said.

"You mustn't let Anthea bully you. She's absolutely ruthless when it comes to Brunswick Lodge and people who've just retired are thin on the ground at the moment. A lot of the volunteers are getting on a bit and don't have the energy they used to have, so new blood, as it were, is irresistible as far as Anthea is concerned."

He smiled again, a rather charming smile that went with an easy manner.

"Actually, she's right. It is a good way of getting to know people, plunging in at the deep end, you might say."

"Do you know anyone in Taviscombe?" I asked. "Or have you any connections down here?"

"We used to come here on holiday a lot when I was a child. My father was a great walker and used to love exploring Exmoor. That was the only reason, really. I had to move about a lot because of my job. I just had a base in London. It was all a bit stressful and when I did retire I didn't want to stay there. For a while I couldn't decide where to go and then I remembered how peaceful it was down here—all the open spaces, the moor and the sea . . . Well I just decided. I saw an advertisement for a rather pleasant house just outside Dunster, came down and looked at it and bought it on the spot."

"What did your wife say about that!"

"My wife died some years ago."

"Oh, I'm so sorry."

"It's been quite a while."

"So have you settled in?"

"Yes. I've always had to travel light so there wasn't much extraneous stuff—I'm a great one for throwing things away—and the furniture fitted in very well. So I'm quite straight now."

I thought of Eva's boxes and considered how different people were—though, in my experience, it is usually men who are the greatest hoarders. I remember my late mother-in-law saying tentatively to Peter, when we had been married for many years, that she'd be grateful if he'd move all his old textbooks and school reports from the cupboard on the landing of the family home.

"Well," I said, "welcome to Brunswick Lodge. But, as I said, don't let Anthea bully you."

"Oh," he said, "I think I can manage Anthea."

"And I rather think he can," I said to Rosemary

later on. "He has an air of quiet authority, if you know what I mean. Do you know anything about him?"

"Well, Mother says that her friend Harold Porter says Donald Webster was quite high up in one of the big multinationals. He doesn't know which one yet, but he's working on it."

"Goodness. He must be very well off."

"And a widower," Rosemary said. "Mother's already got him married to half the unattached females in Taviscombe."

"Oh, I think he's quite capable of avoiding designing females. He seems very nice and he's certainly made Anthea happy. Meanwhile I've got to break it to Michael that he's expected to collect that furniture from the Shelbys' on Saturday."

Michael said he had a shoot on Saturday and there was no way he was going to cancel that for Anthea, but Thea (who also drove their ancient and ill-tempered Land Rover) said she'd do it if I'd go with her to lend a hand with the furniture.

The Shelbys are a local family who live in a large house just outside Taviscombe on the edge of Exmoor. I don't know them particularly well but Michael knows Maurice Shelby, who is a fellow solicitor, though his practice is in Taunton.

"I *think* this is the turning," I said doubtfully. "I've only ever been here once when they opened the garden for the Red Cross. Yes, that's right, I remember that farm track on the left."

Alison Shelby watched anxiously as we lifted the

bookcase and table into the Land Rover. "Are you sure you can manage? Oh dear, you shouldn't be doing that. I'm sure it's too heavy for you. I did hope Maurice would be here—he could have done it—but he had to go into the office—something important, I don't know what—but, of course, he would have been only too happy . . . Oh, do be careful—that shelf is slipping! Do let me . . ."

Finally, much impeded by her help, we got everything loaded up but were then obliged to stay for coffee and more lamentations about Maurice's absence.

"I'm exhausted," Thea said when we finally got away.

"She does go on a bit," I agreed.

"When we've dumped this lot, come and have lunch. I've got to collect Alice at the stables and I know she's longing to tell you about the gymkhana."

The auction duly took place and was deemed a great success, even Derek having to admit reluctantly that the sum raised was more than he expected, though still reserving the right to question the use to which it would be put. Anthea was full of praise for Donald Webster, who had, indeed, conducted the whole affair with great competence and flair.

"Such a valuable addition," Anthea said. "We simply must have him on the committee." And, except for a token protest by Maureen Philips, who always resisted any sort of change, it was unanimously agreed.

"He seemed pleased to be asked," I reported to Rosemary, "though I get the feeling that he finds the whole thing highly amusing, which is quite refreshing."

"He's moved his account down here to Jack's firm," Rosemary said. "He said he didn't want to be back and forth to London all the time. I get the impression he really wants to put down roots here. He seems nice. Jack's asked him to dinner next week so I'll let you know what I think."

But before then she rang me. "Well, he's made a conquest of Mother!"

"No! How?"

"You know she was going to the optician on Wednesday—you remember the fuss she made about those new glasses—well, Mr. Melhuish finished earlier than I expected so she was sitting there waiting for me to collect her. *Not* in the best of moods, as you can imagine. Anyway, Donald Webster came in and, while he was waiting for his appointment, he made polite conversation with her. Well, that's not exactly true; he submitted to her usual rigorous cross-examination—you know what she's like with newcomers and Harold only covered the bare details— with enormous good humor and the upshot of it is he's going to tea with her next Monday!"

"Good heavens!"

"I know. When I took her home she was full of it— such an interesting man, a thorough gentleman, such good manners, so rare nowadays—all that. Fussing about whether Elsie should make her special short-bread as well as her coffee and walnut cake. I thought I might be required to be on duty but she seems to want to keep him all to herself. But I've got strict instructions about what flowers to get and how to arrange them when I go there in the morning—in case there are any more instructions, I imagine."

"Oh well, if your mother's taken to him he's made for life in Taviscombe. I long to know how it all goes, and, then, if he's coming to you for dinner . . ."

"About that, I wondered if you'd come too. To make up numbers and you've met him at Brunswick Lodge so you'd be a familiar face."

"I'd love to."

Rosemary reported that Mrs. Dudley remained enchanted with Donald Webster after the tea party. "So, unless he offends her in some tremendous way, which seems unlikely, he'll be in her good books for life. You know she *never* will admit that she's been wrong about anyone."

On the evening of the dinner party I found I was taking extra trouble deciding what to wear and how my hair looked. It's always interesting to meet someone new in Taviscombe, I told myself, and I was curious to find out more about someone who had, obviously, had such an unusual and interesting life. But although Donald (as we were now to call him), with his easy manner and fund of fascinating stories about his experiences all over the world, was the perfect dinner party guest, I found I knew no more about him as a person than I had known before. I was just left with my original impression that, in the nicest possible way, he found Taviscombe and its inhabitants a source of quiet amusement.

Chapter Three

Eva came back from London in good spirits.

"I had a lovely time. Dear Patrick organized a surprise party—all my old friends. I really enjoyed it. And I went to a few exhibitions and a couple of theaters—oh, and Dan took me to the opening of a new restaurant. Such a peculiar place—everything was black and white, probably the food as well, but the lighting was so low you couldn't really tell."

"I bet Dan had fun with that," I said.

"He said it provided a useful theme for his review."

I laughed. "I'm so glad you had a good time."

"I hope it hasn't unsettled you," Rosemary said. "Taviscombe will seem very dull after all that."

"No, actually, I'm quite glad to be back. It *was* lovely, of course, a nice treat. It was fine when Alan was alive, but it's not the sort of life I'd want to have now. So, come on, tell me what's been going on while I was away."

The Christmas concert is generally considered to be one of the high spots in the Brunswick Lodge calendar. People read poems or extracts from Christmassy books and we sing carols—all rather old-fashioned, I suppose, but everyone seems to enjoy it. This year it ended with Donald Webster reading the Henry Williamson account of the Christmas truce in the First World War, followed by Pauline Jacobs playing "Silent Night" on her recorder. It was very moving and, as the final notes died away, there was a long silence, before applause broke out and people crowded around Donald and Pauline in congratulation.

"That was beautiful," Eva said. "Who was that doing the reading?"

"Oh, that was Donald Webster—" Rosemary began, when Anthea, who was passing, broke in to give her usual panegyric on her latest favorite.

"Such an asset—nothing too much trouble—such a wide experience—of *everything*!"

"Goodness," Eva said when Anthea had passed on to chivy Maureen, who was in charge of the refreshments. "She really is keen. Is he such a paragon?"

"All the social graces," Rosemary said. "He's even captivated Mother."

"No! I must meet this amazing man!"

But a little while later, Donald came up to her, carrying a plate.

"Have a mince pie. I don't recommend the ones on the right which, I've been told, are a little *heavy*. Wholemeal flour, apparently. No? I don't blame you—one can have too many mince pies. Actually, this was an excuse to have a word with you."

Eva smiled. "Really?"

"No, seriously, I wanted to tell you how much I admired your late husband. Shall we sit down?"

They moved away and I lost track of the conversation, but Eva told us later that Donald had met Alan—somewhere in South America, she didn't remember where—and they had spent some time together and had got on very well.

"Apparently there'd been some kind of trouble," she said, "something to do with a drugs raid and they'd been in quite a tight corner and Alan had got them out of it. He was full of praise for Alan's coolness and the clever way he managed it all." Her face was alight with pleasure. "It's such a treat to hear something new about Alan that I've never heard before!"

"He never told you? I'd have thought something like that . . ."

She smiled. "I know, but that sort of thing was run-of-the-mill to Alan, all part of the job. I used to pester him for every detail at first, but I suppose I just got used to it."

"There may be some reference to it in his papers," I said.

"Donald was asking about them. I really must get down to doing something about them."

Anthea suddenly appeared with Alison Shelby in tow, introduced her to Eva and darted away toward the kitchen muttering something about mulled wine.

"I've *so* wanted to meet you," Alison began, "such an admirer of your wonderful husband—Anthea has told us all about him. Maurice always has the news on, never misses it, and we always say we can't imagine how people *could*—be so brave, I mean. When they don't have to, that is. After all they're not soldiers, are they, and they only have those jacket things when all that is going on around them. I know we have to see those terrible things—though sometimes I wonder if we really do—and television is wonderful. A window on the world, I always say. Oh here's Maurice, he'll tell you . . ."

Maurice Shelby approached, shook hands formally with Eva and expressed his admiration for Alan's work in more measured tones.

"It was a job he loved," Eva said. "He wouldn't have been happy doing anything else."

"He was a very brave man," Maurice said, "and a really excellent reporter. A collection of his broadcasts would make a most interesting book. Is anything being considered?"

"There are a lot of his papers that need to be

sorted—at present in my garage—I do intend to do something about them soon."

He nodded. "I will look forward very much to seeing something in print. And now you have moved down here. Do you have connections in the area?"

"My parents lived just outside Porlock. They're both dead now, of course, but I was born and brought up here."

"I wonder if I knew them?"

"My family name is Benson."

"Really?" he thought for a moment. "The name doesn't ring a bell. And do you have any close family here?"

"I was an only child. Rosemary here's a sort of second or third cousin—but that's all."

"Well, I hope you have settled in well and are happy here."

He bowed slightly and, gathering up his wife who showed signs of wanting to continue the conversation, moved away.

"Goodness," Eva said when they were out of earshot, "what an unusual man."

"Old-fashioned," Rosemary said. "I always feel he should be wearing a stiff wing collar and pince-nez."

"He's got a single practice in Taunton—at least he's on his own now. He had a partner, who went abroad somewhere. I can't imagine how he deals with modern things like computers, timed interviews and all the stuff they have to cope with these days. But Michael, who knows him quite well, says he's very much on the ball, so I suppose that formal manner is just a façade."

Rosemary glanced toward the kitchen where Maureen and Anthea were emerging, each carrying a tray of glasses.

"Do we really want to sample Maureen's mulled wine," she said, "or shall we slip quietly away and have a real drink?"

A few weeks later, I'd just opened the back door to dispel the smell of Foss's fish (why does fish for an animal, even if very expensive and of a high quality, smell quite different from fish meant for humans?) when the telephone rang.

"Sheila, can you come over to Eva's? Something's happened."

"What?"

"There's been a fire in her garage."

"Is she all right?"

"Yes, just a bit shaken. I thought we should rally round."

"Of course, I'll be right over."

When I got to the cottage there was a smell of burning in the air and the grass verge of the lane was churned up, presumably by the fire engine. The garage door was shut and blackened, but there was no other sign of damage.

"What happened?" I asked as Eva poured coffee for us all.

"I'd gone to bed and was asleep when something woke me—a noise in the lane, I thought. You know how it is if you wake up when you've just gone to sleep, sort of disoriented. But then I smelled burning. So I got up and looked out of the window. I couldn't see anything—it was pitch-black—so I thought I'd better go down and check things. When I opened the front door I saw smoke coming out of the garage, so I phoned the fire brigade and, fortunately, they came very quickly and put it out before too much damage was done."

"How awful for you!" I said.

"It all happened so quickly I didn't really take in what was happening until it was all over."

"But frightening. Thank goodness the fire brigade came so quickly. Do they know what started it?"

"Not really. They said there was no immediately apparent cause. I got the impression it was some electrical fault."

"I must say," Rosemary broke in, "I didn't like the look of that bulb hanging from the ceiling on what looked like a very old flex. I think you should have the wiring in the cottage checked. You can't be too careful."

"I thought the surveyor had all that sorted," Eva said. "But," she went on quickly, "it wouldn't hurt to have that nice electrician you found me have a look at it."

"Was there much damage inside?" I asked. "How about the papers; were they all right?"

"Fortunately they were at *this* end of the garage—the light fitting's up near the door."

"You really must get them sorted," Rosemary said.

"Or at least bring them indoors. That garage door is badly burned and I bet you haven't got the padlock on it!"

"Well, no. But, honestly, I really can't imagine why anyone would want to steal them."

"It's not just stealing. There's a lot of vandalism about. There were a couple of cases in the *Free Press* lately—children destroying things. *And* in one case they'd burned a barn down."

"Oh, but that was quite different," I protested. "They were playing in there and it was a Dutch barn, wide open, and during the day, not in the middle of the night."

"Oh well, it's done now," Eva said. "Could have been much worse. I'll get a new door and have the electric light seen to."

However Rosemary insisted on moving the papers to a place of safety, so we spent the next few mornings transferring them, and the filing cabinets, to the spare room.

"Oh dear," Eva said, looking round the now over-crowded room, "there's no way I could have any-one to stay. I suppose I ought to get rid of those books—the ones I couldn't make my mind up about—and see what I can do with all these." She gestured despairingly at the filing cabinets now lining the walls and taking up an inordinate amount of room so that it was almost impossible to get through the door.

"There's just one more lot of papers," Rosemary

said encouragingly. "I'll just go and bring them up from the garage."

Eva sighed. "It's very good of Rosemary . . ." she began.

"But you wish she wouldn't?" I said.

"Well, yes. I feel dreadfully ungrateful, and I know I've got to get down to things sometime, but for now I wish I could just *be*."

"It's early days yet. Rosemary, bless her, has always been a one for getting things sorted.

"And it's just as well someone does otherwise nothing would ever get done. Anyway, she's always had to because of her mother."

Mrs. Dudley was a great one for getting things done—usually by other people. "Never put off till tomorrow," she would say impressively, as if it was a completely original thought, "what you can do today."

"I think," Eva said, "she feels responsible for me, being a sort of relative. I don't mean that's the only reason, but she's always had a strong feeling about family."

"Just like her mother," I said. "Though don't tell her I said that!"

Christmas came and went. I spent it with the children and Eva was with Rosemary and Jack

"Dan and Patrick don't do Christmas," she said in response to my inquiry. "They sit around in their dressing gowns and eat boiled eggs."

Donald Webster continued to contribute to the proceedings at Brunswick Lodge.

"I thought he might be sick of it by now," Rosemary said. "Being bossed around by Anthea."

"I don't think he is," I said. "It seems to me he only does what he wants to do, and always with that half-amused attitude, as if he thinks it's all a bit of a joke."

"Harold says he worked for one of the big American multinationals, chemicals and things. Apparently he ran their main South American operation, whatever that might mean."

"Goodness. He must have been important. Odd that he should have ended up in Taviscombe. I mean, I know he said it was because of his childhood holidays, but, really, when he had the whole world to choose from—"

"There's nothing wrong with Taviscombe," Rosemary said sharply. "Area of outstanding natural beauty and all that."

"Yes, I know," I said thoughtfully. "But he never seems to go for walks or drives, doesn't appear at all keen on the outdoor kind of things. In fact, he spends most of his time here, at Brunswick Lodge. Why would he choose to help with coffee mornings in a small seaside town after the life he's been used to?"

"Nice and restful after all that time abroad." Rosemary doesn't have a very high opinion of abroad.

"And those tea parties with your mother."

"I agree that's odd. But perhaps he collects characters."

"Yes," I said, "you might call Anthea and your mother characters. But after all this time, what is it— several months now—you'd think he'd be bored . . ." I shook my head. "I don't know—there's something about him that doesn't add up."

"Never mind, let's make the most of him while we can. Anthea's never been so little trouble since he came and Mother's taken on a new lease of life. He drove her out to that place at Exford for lunch the other day. And you know how she said she couldn't *possibly* manage a car journey that far when I suggested it ages ago!"

"He certainly has charm. And a subtle kind of charm, nothing obvious or over the top. Everyone likes him. Even Derek said that Donald's the only person who's ever appreciated just how complicated the finances of Brunswick Lodge really are."

I was on my hands and knees scrubbing a stain on the carpet in the dining room when there was a ring at the front door. Wondering why my animals never chose to be sick in the kitchen, which is tiled and easier to clean, I hurried to answer the bell which was being rung again with some urgency. It was Rosemary.

"Whatever's happened?" I asked as she hurried inside.

She made for the kitchen, which is where we usually chat, and sat down at the table, looking quite agitated.

"It's Eva."

"What is it? Is she all right?"

"Donald Webster's asked her out to dinner!"

"So?"

"At the Castle in Taunton."

"Lucky her," I said enviously. "So what's the fuss about?"

"Well, don't you think it's significant?"

"Significant of what?"

"Oh, for goodness' sake, Sheila. You don't take just anyone to the Castle. It sounds like a *date*!"

"Not necessarily so. I mean, they're both used to what Dan would call fine dining. Where else would he take her?" I said. "I'll put the kettle on."

Rosemary laughed ruefully. "You think I'm being ridiculous?"

"Well . . ."

"It's just that when she told me she seemed excited and, well, I remembered what you said about him, and I was worried for her."

"And as for it being a date, as you call it, he probably just wants to talk to her about Alan."

"You're right, of course. It's just that she's family and I feel responsible for her."

"And even if it is a date, Eva's perfectly able to look after herself. Here, have a biscuit."

"But she's in a vulnerable state at the moment and I would hate her to be hurt. Donald Webster is a bit too charming, if you ask me." She bit into the biscuit. "You said yourself there's something fishy about him."

"I didn't say fishy, exactly. But, honestly, Eva's

been out in the world long enough to know what's what."

"Yes, of course, I'm being stupid. It's just that I was taken by surprise." She took another biscuit. "What I'm not looking forward to is Mother finding out that he's taking Eva to the Castle when he only took *her* to that place at Exford."

Chapter Four

A few days later, I was sitting in the Buttery when Eva came and sat down beside me.

"Great minds think alike," she said as she put her cup of hot chocolate down next to mine.

"The only thing on a horrible day like this! And I got a Danish pastry. I shouldn't really, but I couldn't resist."

Eva has diabetes, has done for years, but it never seems to restrict her diet. That's another thing Rosemary worries about.

"Did you have a gorgeous pudding at the Castle?" I asked. "I believe they do really super ones."

"Well, I did have a chocolate thing but it was quite small."

"Was it a good evening?"

"Yes, it was." She smiled. "A really good evening."

"Did Donald want to tell you about Alan and their tight spot?"

"For a bit, but really we just talked. He's the most interesting man, been everywhere, seen everything, met the most extraordinary people."

"Like Alan."

She nodded. "Oh, Sheila, I do love being down here—I wouldn't want to live anywhere else—but sometimes, just sometimes, I do miss it all. For goodness' sake don't tell Rosemary, but I miss the—the *buzz*, not just Alan, though of course that's the worst, but just the feeling of being at the center of things, of conversations that aren't just—well, you know . . ."

"Parochial. You miss the great metropolis. Of course you do. And Donald comes from the same world."

She nodded again. "Exactly."

"Well, good for you. Does he feel the same way? He seems to have settled down here very comfortably— all that stuff at Brunswick Lodge. I thought he might have become bored with it by now, but he doesn't seem to be."

"No, I think he really has settled. He didn't say why, but I think he was quite glad to leave South America."

"It sounds as if it must have been a great responsibility."

"That's what I thought. He didn't talk much about his actual job—I gather there'd been some major disagreement—but we had so much else in common, the time really flew by."

"Are you going to see him again?"

"He said something about getting tickets for this thing at the Theatre Royal in Bath."

"That would be nice," I said, thinking that Rosemary would be quite hurt, remembering that Eva had turned down her offer of that particular treat.

"Yes, it would be fun. It's ages since I went to a theater." I didn't remind her that she'd been to several theaters with Dan and Patrick when she was in London, but, I thought, this was different. Looking at her animated face and hearing the lively tone of her voice I decided that, yes, it obviously was quite different.

Thinking about it when I got home, I decided I was glad for Eva. It really had been a massive change of lifestyle for her and it was natural that she should be drawn to someone from her old world. I still wasn't sure what I thought about Donald. Like everyone else, I had felt his charm, and, although I instinctively mistrusted it, I had absolutely no reason to do so. He was probably just a really nice, sociable man. But, then, he had risen to a very prominent position in a very large international corporation, and I felt, also instinctively, that really nice men didn't achieve that sort of thing. Those who did had other qualities, less agreeable. But, I reminded myself, Eva had lived in that world. As I told Rosemary, she was perfectly capable of looking after herself. And, really, it was quite natural that Donald, in a small town like Taviscombe, should turn to someone he had so much in common with. But, oh dear, if Eva did go out with, take up with—what was the suitable phrase?—Donald Webster, Rosemary *would* be upset, and I hated the thought of her being hurt by what she might feel was Eva's desertion.

Donald must have moved quite swiftly because tickets for the Theatre Royal in Bath duly arrived.

"It's for the pre-London run of *Heartbreak House*," Eva told us enthusiastically. "It's got a marvelous cast. It was so clever of Donald to get tickets—it's pretty well sold out."

"How splendid," I said. "It's such a gorgeous theater," I went on hastily to cover up Rosemary's lack of response, "and they have such terrific things on there and it's not really that far away, but I never seem to do anything about it. Silly, really."

"Next time there's anything special on, we must *all* go," Eva said.

Anthea had stopped badgering Eva to give a talk at Brunswick Lodge since Donald had proved an easier target.

"South America is such a fascinating place," she was saying, "and we none of us know anything at all about it. It's a real privilege to have someone like Donald, who held a very high position out there, to tell us all about it."

"He's only going to talk about the country," Derek cut in. "More a sort of travelog."

"Well, it's all going to be most interesting," Anthea responded.

"I didn't say it wasn't going to be interesting,"

Derek said. "Donald is a very interesting man and whatever he has to say will be worth listening to. Unlike that woman who went on about Corfe Castle, who you said was so wonderful. Hardly anyone turned up for that. We should have a full house for Donald and I reckon we could easily charge five pounds for him."

"With refreshments," Maureen said. And the conversation turned to who was going to bring what and wasn't it time something was done about the tea urn.

Donald's talk was, indeed, interesting, very lively and full of anecdotes and people crowded around him at the end as he most amiably continued to answer questions.

"Well, really." Alison Shelby was at my elbow. "I don't know when I've heard such a good talk! So interesting; it really brought it all to life, didn't it? Such an amazing place. Mind you, I can't say I'd like to live there—give me England all the time—and the people! Well, I suppose it takes all sorts, but some of the things . . ." She moved past me and managed to insinuate herself into the group around Donald where she continued her enthusiastic exclamations.

"It was certainly very popular." A cool voice behind me. I turned and saw that it was Maurice Shelby.

"It was," I agreed. "Most entertaining, and he really knew his subject."

"Indeed. Since he spent many years out there and traveled widely. His job seems to have taken him to many different places."

"Actually, he didn't really mention his job," I said tentatively.

"No, I suppose it would have been unsuitable to do so."

"You mean because it was a large multinational company—you think there may be a lot of things he can't talk about?"

"Possibly. I don't know the terms of his contract, but I imagine there must have been some restrictions."

"I suppose so," I said reluctantly, "but I'd have thought in a talk like this it would have been all right to say something—just to give us a general idea of what he did exactly."

"Apparently he chose not to do so. And now, if you will excuse me, I need to collect my wife." He glanced toward the group where Alison was still in full flow, moving purposefully toward her, and I reflected that Mr. and Mrs. Bennet still lived today. Certainly she had the remains of a certain kind of prettiness which accounted for the match, but their two daughters (who took after their father) had managed their marriages (one to a doctor who would, one day, certainly be a consultant, and one to a barrister who, one day, would inevitably be a judge) most competently themselves.

I went into the kitchen to help with the refreshments. Rosemary was buttering bread for sandwiches and I began to slice a cucumber.

"What did you think?" she asked.

"Very good. Most entertaining."

"Not much about himself, though. Or his job—I should think that's what most people wanted to know."

"Maurice Shelby thinks there may have been something in his contract that didn't allow him to," I said.

Rosemary looked up, her buttery knife suspended. "That sounds sinister, you must admit. And it's not as though he was going to tell us about secret formulas or whatever."

"Oh, I expect it's just standard when you get to that sort of position. How much of this cucumber do you want?"

"No, but you must admit—" She broke off as Maureen came into the kitchen and began fiddling with the tea urn.

"Wasn't it a splendid talk?" she said. "Such a pity Eva couldn't make it. She'd really have enjoyed it." Eva was spending a few days in London with Dan and Patrick. "Though I suppose," she went on, "she's probably heard most of it already, being as she's *such* a friend of Mr. Webster. Do you know, until we can get this thing fixed properly, we'd be better off boiling a couple of kettles."

"You see," Rosemary said later, "people are beginning to talk. Mother was saying only the other day that Vera Davis saw them having lunch together in Taunton."

"They're friends, for goodness' sake. Why shouldn't they have lunch together!"

"Mother thought it was unsuitable—it's not that long since Alan died."

"Well, you know what your mother and her friends are like."

But Rosemary, who any other time would have laughed at the whole thing, seemed to be taking it seriously and I hoped that her concern for Eva wouldn't make things awkward between them.

Eva rang me when she got back from London.

"Sheila, have I done something to upset Rosemary?"

"Not that I know of. Why do you ask?"

"She's being a bit distant, if you know what I mean."

"Oh dear."

"What?"

I took a deep breath. "I'm sure she doesn't mean to be—it's just that she's worried about you and doesn't know how to say anything."

There was silence for a moment, then Eva said, "Is it about Donald?"

"Yes, well, in a way. Her mother—well you know how old-fashioned she is—seemed to think—"

"That I shouldn't go out with anyone now I'm a widow." She gave a sort of laugh. "I'd forgotten what Taviscombe was like. People are talking?"

"As you say—people in Taviscombe—"

"And does Rosemary feel the same?" she asked.

"Of *course* not," I said hastily.

"She doesn't really like Donald, does she?"

"No, it's not that; it's just that he's rather different from people we're used to down here."

"Oh, come off it, Sheila. You've been out in the big wide world!"

"Yes, I have, but Rosemary is very Taviscombe orientated—you know that—and she's not quite sure what to make of him. It's just that she's very protective of you—family and all that—and doesn't want you to be hurt."

Eva sighed. "Oh dear, I do hope things aren't going to be awkward. I like Donald, I like him very much, and I really don't want to stop seeing him. Do you think I should?"

"Certainly not. Just tell Rosemary how you feel. Clear the air and everything will be fine."

But soon after that, Rosemary had another thing to worry about.

"That wretched man," she said, "has been pestering Eva again."

"What wretched man?"

"Robert Butler—you know, the man who has the farm just down the road from her."

"Oh yes, I know who you mean. How's he been pestering her?"

"Well, you know he wants to bring water across her field."

Eva has a fair-sized field behind the garden—it's part of the property—and Rosemary has always been full of dire warnings about it—"You'll have to see to the hedges, and who's going to cut the hay? It's going to be nothing but trouble."

"Is that such a big deal? I mean he'll have to pay for it. Why does he need extra water anyway?"

"It's for a caravan park he wants to open."

"No! How awful."

"You see, I was right about that field. I did warn her to get rid of it straightaway."

"If she had," I pointed out, "whoever bought it might have given permission straightaway."

"That's as may be," Rosemary brushed it aside. "It seems that field is the only way the water can be brought to the particular bit of his land that's suitable."

"Has he got planning permission for this caravan park?" I asked.

"He's thick as thieves with half the council so *that* won't be a problem once he gets the water."

"Oh dear."

"He's offered her a lot of money, but you know Eva, if she's made up her mind about something. And there's no way she'd want a place like that next door—think of all the traffic back and forth up the lane!"

"She really could do without this hassle. But you're right—she'll stand firm."

And when I saw her next she was quite determined.

"It's just the sort of situation Alan would have hated," she said. "I feel I'd be letting him down if I gave in, even if I wanted to, which I don't!"

"What does Donald say about it all?" I asked.

"Oh, he's had to go to Chicago for a bit—something

the company he worked for wants to consult him about. I don't know the details, but I think he's likely to be away for several weeks."

"That's a shame; I'm sure he would have been very supportive."

"Oh well, there's nothing this Butler man can do as long as I keep saying no."

Rosemary, when I told her about the conversation, pounced on the fact of Donald's trip to Chicago.

"I wonder what *that*'s all about."

"Something his firm wanted to consult him about," I suggested. "Something about the South American operation that he'd know about."

"It sounds a bit odd. I mean, they've got people out there, haven't they? Why do they need him?"

"Presumably because it's something connected with the time he was out there."

"It must be important," Rosemary continued, "if they've got him flying all the way across the Atlantic."

"I don't think flying across the Atlantic is a very big deal to people like Donald."

"But," she persisted, "why would they ask him if he'd left under some sort of cloud?"

"I don't think that was the case," I said. "Eva said there'd been a disagreement."

"A *major* disagreement."

"Whatever. But there's no reason to think it was anything sinister."

"Well, I do think Eva should be careful. After all, we know very little about him."

"Honestly, I do think Eva's capable of looking after herself."

"Mother says she's in a very vulnerable position so soon after Alan's death. And I'm inclined to agree with her."

I sighed. The fact that Rosemary said that she agreed with one of her mother's opinions really did indicate just how worried she was about her cousin.

Chapter Five

"That really was most interesting," I said reluctantly. Anthea had been going on for ages about this genealogist and how lucky we were that *she* had got hold of him for Brunswick Lodge.

"Quite a coup," Anthea was saying. "He's very much in demand, you know, gives talks all over the country."

"What a pity he had to leave so early to get his train," Alison Shelby said. "There were such a lot of things I wanted to ask him." She turned to Eva. "Don't you agree—it was absolutely fascinating?"

"I must say it did make me think," Eva said. "I've always wanted to know more about the family. I don't know much about either side, my father's or my mother's. My father never talked about his family in Australia and I expect it would be difficult to find stuff there, but *his* father came from round here and I'd really like to know about them."

"And there are so many ways you can find out," Alison broke in. "All those places on the Internet—not that I've ever been able to make head or tail of computers—Maurice looks after that side of things!"

"I think I might give it a go," Eva said. "And my mother's family too. Her maiden name was Lydia Castel—quite an unusual name, which might help."

"Oh do!" Alison said enthusiastically. "And you must let us know how you get on. Who knows what you might find, though perhaps you might not want to know—all those people on television discovering their ancestors were murderers or ended up in the workhouse. I always say—"

"Alison," Maurice Shelby broke in, "we really should be going. I'm expecting an important call and I need to be home to take it."

"Yes, of course, dear, I'll just get my coat. I took it off when I came in—the room was so hot. I *think* I left it in the lobby."

Her husband raised his eyebrows slightly but made no comment, following his wife who was still wondering where she might have left her coat.

"Have you ever investigated your family?" I asked Donald Webster, who had been to the talk—sitting next to Eva and deep in conversation with her as usual, which had caused Maureen to give me what she would have called one of her Looks.

"No," he replied. "My family lived in Zimbabwe

for several generations, when it was Rhodesia, that is. They were farmers and left when things got difficult over there. So there wouldn't be any records here."

"I'm so sorry," I said. "It must have been awful."

"I'd already left by then. Off to get a job that would let me see the world."

"I suppose you might be able to find your more remote ancestors," I suggested. "You know, before they went to Africa."

"That might be fun," Eva said. "We could tackle all those websites together. I'm sure you're better at that sort of thing than I am."

"I'd be delighted to give you a hand," he said, "but I'm not sure I want to investigate my lot. Like Alison said, you never know what you might find!"

I didn't see Eva for a while to find out how she got on. I had a difficult review article to write about a book written by a friend which, while full of excellent research, I found almost totally unreadable. So I shut myself away to wrestle with it.

When I emerged, I asked Rosemary how Eva was.

"I saw her yesterday," Rosemary said. "She certainly seems very absorbed with this genealogy thing."

"Has she made any progress?"

"Not really. She says it's all very complicated, going through endless census things, especially when you don't have much to go on."

"She never asked her mother about the family?"

"No, well, you don't, do you? You think they'll always be there, and by the time you want to ask, it's too late."

"I don't really remember much about her. Do you?"

"Not a lot. Well, with Eva away at school I only saw her parents occasionally in the holidays, and my parents didn't see them often. Mother quite liked Uncle Richard (in spite of his being an Australian) but she didn't approve of Aunt Lydia (I always called them Aunt and Uncle, though of course they weren't) for some reason—I can't remember the ins and outs of it. You know what Mother's like—it's usually something quite irrational."

"I only met them a couple of times. I remember being impressed by the fact that he was the first Australian I'd ever met—an interesting man, and she was very nice, very warm and friendly. And I'd never known anyone called Lydia before. It's an unusual name, though I suppose it might be a family name. Oh well, I suppose Eva may find out—that is, unless she finds it all too difficult and gives up."

"Not with Donald Webster round there urging her on."

"Oh, I see." I hesitated for a minute. "Well, he did say he'd help."

"Any excuse."

"Oh, come on, Rosemary," I said coaxingly. "Is it so very bad? He seems a nice enough chap and they do get on very well; they've got a lot in common, after all."

"I suppose so," she said reluctantly. "Perhaps I've

been a bit unfair. But it's only been a short time since Alan died . . ."

"Nearly a year. And Eva's so much happier since she's been seeing Donald. I'm sure Alan would want her to be happy."

"Yes, you're right. I'm probably making a fuss about nothing. It's just that he's so *charming*!"

"I know what you mean, but it's not fair to condemn him for being nice to people."

Rosemary told me that Dan and Patrick were coming to stay for a few days. Dan was doing an article about new (and expensive) restaurants in the West Country and they were calling in on Eva on their way down to Cornwall where, apparently, the most glamorous ones were to be found.

"I'd really like to see Dan again," Rosemary said, "so I've invited them to supper, and Eva, of course, and I hope you'll come too."

"I'd love to. I've always wanted to meet Dan and Patrick. But isn't it brave of you to invite them to a *meal*?"

"Oh, I specifically said supper and not dinner. And, actually, Dan is very tolerant of what he calls 'proper cooking'—not a bit what you'd expect from his reviews."

"What will you give him?"

"Sausages and mash, by special request—he's very keen on our local sausages. Eva once took him some as a present. And apple crumble."

"It sounds delicious."

"I did think of asking Donald Webster too, but I thought perhaps Eva would rather introduce him to Dan separately, if you see what I mean."

Dan, tall and shambling, was wearing jeans and a T-shirt with the legend "Most Cooks Spoil the Broth." His dark hair flopped over his forehead, almost obscuring the gold-rimmed spectacles he wore balanced halfway down his large nose—Alan's nose. Patrick, on the other hand, was small and neat, with smootheddown fair hair. He wore a well-cut dark suit and a very handsome silk tie.

"So you haven't found any suitable restaurants in this part of the West Country?" I asked Dan.

He shook his head. "No, thank goodness. It remains pure and unsullied. Like these delicious sausages." He smiled at Rosemary. "No, I'm delighted to say that the tradition of proper cooking still holds sway. The occasional gastropub pops up from time to time, but they never last long. But, please, don't let's spoil this splendid occasion by talking about such things." He turned to me. "I greatly enjoyed your book on Mrs. Gaskell and there's so much I want to ask you about the novels of the period. Where, for instance, would you place Mrs. Oliphant? Personally I found *Salem Chapel* a quite remarkable book."

He then embarked on a survey of the Victorian novel, obviously based on such an extensive knowledge of the genre that I found I had to dig deep to match it. We disagreed over some authors ("You must admit that Mrs. Cholmondeley's *Red Pottage* is exceptional") but came together over a mutual passion for Charlotte Yonge ("A complete page-turner if ever there was one"). We parted reluctantly at the end of the evening with a promise on my part to send him a spare edition I had of *The Monthly Packet*.

"You and Dan certainly got on well," Rosemary said.

"Oh well, when you get two people obsessed with the same author . . ." I replied.

"He's a very kind person underneath that rather peculiar manner. He's devoted to Eva—he was wonderful when Alan died. I don't think she could have coped without him and Patrick."

"I didn't have a chance, really, to talk to Patrick. What's he like? He didn't say very much."

"He never does, but *when* he does it's always something to the point. He sits there taking everything in. He's very good at summing people up."

"Do we know what he thought about Donald? I imagine Eva introduced him to both of them. How did they get on?"

"Eva seemed pleased," Rosemary said. "I gather it was all quite easy and casual."

"Did Dan know how much they'd been seeing each other?"

"Oh, I think so."

"So everything's fine? I mean, if Dan approves."

"I suppose so."

"And Patrick?"

"I think he said something vague and impersonal."

"Well, that's all right, then."

"Yes, of course it is," Rosemary said. "I'm sorry, Sheila—I've been a bore about this Donald thing." She thought for a moment and then went on, "I think I was jealous. You know, when Eva came back down here it was lovely to see her again and I suppose I rather took over her life—well, she is family—and I sort of resented it when Donald suddenly became such a part of it. Then Mother kept going on about how short a time it was since Alan died. Of course *she* was jealous because Donald wasn't paying as much attention to her. All absolutely ridiculous!"

"Eva's a big girl now," I said. "And she hasn't exactly led a sheltered life."

"I know. I'm an idiot."

"I can see how you felt—she really is a rather special person."

For a town house, Brunswick Lodge has quite a big garden. Sheltered by high brick walls, it's been lovingly planted and cared for by a team of passionate gardeners and, once a year, they grudgingly allow us to have a garden party. Like everything else, this is the source of considerable friction, the gardeners' committee placing every obstacle they can think of in the way of the general committee's plans. Naturally Anthea tries to pull rank ("Enid Williams has absolutely no idea of organization—if things were left to her the whole thing would be a complete shambles!"), but Enid is equally strong-minded. She knows that just once a year she has the upper hand.

"Of course we have to have the little tables on the

lawn," Anthea said. "It's ridiculous to say they will damage the grass. Anyone with a grain of common sense would realize that there's no way they could go on the paths."

"No," I agreed, "the paths are much too uneven and, anyway, if the tables were there people would have to walk about on the grass much more."

"Exactly!" Anthea said triumphantly. "Now then, do we have tablecloths on them? Last year, if you remember, it was very windy and the cloths kept blowing about. No," she went on, answering her own question as she frequently did, "better not; besides, people tend to spill things on them and then there are all the laundry costs."

"What are we doing about the urn?" Maureen Philips broke in. "If it rains like last year I don't want to have to carry it in—it was really quite dangerous and if Derek hadn't lent me a hand I don't know how we would have managed."

"No, no," Anthea said impatiently. "You remember we said we'd have iced tea and iced coffee and have it all done in the kitchen."

"I still think," Maureen replied stubbornly, "that a lot of people would like a nice cup of tea."

"Well, if they actually *ask* for one," Anthea said irritably, "Sheila can make them one in the kitchen."

I had resigned myself to spending a lot of the garden party in the kitchen since I'd rashly offered to make the iced tea from a splendid recipe given to me by an American friend. I wasn't entirely sorry because the garden party often took place in unsuitable weather and it was no small thing, at such a time, to be warm and dry.

Unusually, the day dawned to bright sunshine and showed every sign of being A Perfect Day For It, as everyone said as they crowded out into the garden. There was no peace, however, in the kitchen as Anthea kept putting her head round the door with new instructions and comments.

"Was it really necessary to actually *buy* all that ice from the supermarket, Sheila? Surely people could have brought some from their own refrigerators."

I murmured meekly that it made things easier and that I'd paid for it myself.

"I don't think we should take the sandwiches and sausage rolls out yet—the sun is really quite strong and will spoil them."

"How many people are there now?" I asked. "They'll be wanting food."

"Quite a few, but they seem to be hanging about inside—I'd better go and move them on."

She rushed off, leaving the door open as usual. A buzz of conversation indicated that she hadn't been successful in chivying people outside.

"So," Alison was saying, "how far have you got?"

"Not very," Eva said, laughing. "I kept getting sidetracked—all sorts of fascinating stuff in those census things. And Donald wasn't much help; he was just as bad, haring off after unusual names."

"But you must persevere," Alison said enthusiastically. "We're all longing to know how it turns out. I wanted Maurice to do ours, but he said he didn't

have the time and, of course, I'd be absolutely useless. Well," she continued proudly, "I wouldn't even
know how to switch the computer on. I'm an absolute
duffer at anything mechanical. Maurice will tell you—
the trouble I've had with the tumble dryer . . ."

"I think we're required outside," Maurice Shelby
said drily, and just then Anthea returned and shep-
herded them firmly into the garden.

I'd squeezed some lemons and was just fishing
out the pips when I heard Donald's voice.

"Thank goodness they've gone. There's something
I want to talk to you about."

"What is it?" Eva replied.

"Not here. Can we go somewhere after this is
finished?"

"Yes, of course. Come back to the cottage and have
a drink—we're going to need one by then." There was
a pause, then she said, "You look very serious—what
is it?"

"Later. I'll tell you later."

The voices died away and I finished making the
lemon tea.

Chapter Six

"It seems like such a good opportunity," Rosemary said. "Jilly's taking some things that Delia says she wants in Oxford and I've been longing to see her room and how she's settled in. And St. Hilda's is such an interesting college, with the river and everything."

"It sounds lovely," I said. "How long will you be away?"

"We thought we'd take a whole week. I've always wanted to see Blenheim and we might be able to get tickets for a matinee at Stratford . . ."

"Good for you. You haven't had a proper holiday for ages and it will be nice for you and Jilly to spend some time together. What about Mark and Jack?"

"Mark's going to stay with a school friend and

Jack says he can fend for himself. I'll leave lots of things in the freezer, but I expect he'll live on fish and chips and takeaways. Actually, I think he's quite looking forward to having the house to himself and doing what he wants to do when he wants to do it."

"Where are you staying?"

"There's what sounds like rather a nice little hotel in Summertown. Jilly found it on the Internet, which is how people seem to do things now."

"I'm sure it'll be lovely." I paused and then asked the inevitable question. "What about your mother?"

Rosemary laughed. "*Such* a good idea. Something she's always wanted to do, but, of course, she's only a poor old woman and things like that are impossible for her, though, naturally, if someone had *asked* her, she would have made every effort and it would have been such a treat, since *she* never has the chance to leave the house these days. But she quite understands that the young are all so busy with their own lives that they don't have time for old people. They'll understand when *they're* old. Don't worry about me, I'll be fine, you go and enjoy yourself . . . etc., etc."

"Oh dear."

"Oh, it's only what I expected and I'm certainly not going to let it spoil things for me."

"I'll keep an eye on things and call round and let her tell me how selfish the young are if you like."

"Bless you, she'll love that."

"You go off and have a lovely time and don't worry about anything."

* * *

A few days after Rosemary left, I phoned her mother. Elsie, her housekeeper, answered, which was unusual, since Mrs. Dudley usually kept a firm control over that particular instrument.

"I'm afraid she's really quite poorly," Elsie said. "I called the surgery, but, of course now Dr. Macdonald's retired she doesn't care for any of the other doctors. It's really very awkward. Still, I spoke to Dr. Porter—he's the one I go to—and he was very nice. He said he'd come round—we're only a few minutes away—which was very good of him. You know how they don't visit these days, but he could tell that I was worried. Anyway, he did come and he was very good with her. He says she's got this gastric thing that's going round, very nasty it is. Lots of fluids, he said, and to keep warm and stay in bed. Like I said, he was really very nice. And he'll come later in the week, but said to call him if she wasn't any better."

"Oh dear," I said. "I'm so sorry. Is there anything I can do? Shall I call round?"

"No, dear, there's nothing you can do and I think she'd rather you waited until she feels better—you know what I mean."

I did know. Mrs. Dudley never cared for visitors unless she was feeling (and looking) her best.

"I quite understand. Have you been in touch with Rosemary?"

"I did suggest it but she said she wouldn't dream of

spoiling her holiday." I could imagine the exact martyred tone in which this was uttered. "And really, Mrs. Malory, I think she just wants to be quiet. You know how it is when you don't feel a hundred percent."

"Of course. Well, give her my love and mind you look after yourself."

"Oh, I'm all right—I never catch anything and nothing ever bothers me."

I reflected that, after all her years with Mrs. Dudley, it would take something positively cataclysmic to ruffle Elsie.

After having done my duty by Mrs. Dudley, I thought Rosemary would expect me to see how Eva was. And, actually, I was curious about the conversation with Donald that I'd overheard at the garden party. What, I wondered, was the serious thing he wanted to talk to her about? Eva was quite a long time answering the phone and I thought she was out, and when she did answer, she didn't seem herself.

"It's this wretched gastric thing," she said when I inquired. "Apparently there's a lot of it about. Well, that's what Mrs. Mac said." Mrs. Mac is her cleaner and a great one for stating the obvious.

"Oh dear, how horrible. Is there anything I can do? Shall I come round?"

"That's sweet of you but there's nothing I need. I've been up and down all night and I feel a bit wobbly and just want to go back to bed."

"What about your prescription?"

"No, I'm all right for everything at the moment

and, as you can imagine, I don't feel like any food. I just want to crawl away and be by myself."

"Well, take care and do ring if there's anything I can do."

But the next day I was incapable of doing anything. Whatever it was that was going round had caught up with me and it was as much as I could do to cope with the animals, who never seem to understand about human illness. The next few days were very unpleasant and I was really grateful to Thea who came in to see to Tris and Foss and supply me with the lots of fluids that Dr. Horobin had prescribed for Mrs. Dudley. But, on the whole, I understood exactly what Eva meant by being on your own.

When I felt well enough to get up and lie on the couch, feeling like a Victorian heroine, pale and interesting, I thought I should inquire after the other two invalids. Mrs. Dudley had resumed control of the telephone and was able to tell me just how ill she had been.

"Dr. Horobin said I must have a wonderful constitution to have made such a good recovery from a bad attack like that at my age. He did say, however, that I must take *especial* care now and take things very slowly. Of course, he'll never be another Dr. Macdonald, but he seems to be very sensible for a young man."

I reflected that, as Elsie said, he had been very good with her. In a brief pause in the conversation I tentatively mentioned that I too had been ill and was still not really able to do much.

"Oh, you young people, no stamina. Dr. Porter said that mine is the last generation who are the real survivors."

Well, that was true at any rate. I rang Eva but there was no reply and I hoped it meant that she was now sufficiently recovered to go out. I still didn't feel well enough to make any effort myself and was looking forward to Rosemary's return and all the news she might bring.

She came back a day early and the news she brought was not what I had expected.

"Oh, Sheila, I had to come round—I couldn't tell you on the phone," she burst out before I could express surprise at her early return.

"What on earth's the matter?"

"It's Eva. She's dead."

"No! How awful. What happened? I know she had this wretched bug but she seemed to be getting over it."

"Mrs. Mac went round to clean as usual. She rang the bell but there was no answer. She thought Eva had gone out but the car was still there. Still, she's got a key so she let herself in. Everything looked normal but then she found Eva in bed . . ." She paused, then went on. "She couldn't rouse her so she called an ambulance and they said she was dead and had been for a couple of days."

"How horrible."

"I know." She was silent for a moment. "Dr. Porter came and there's got to be a postmortem."

"Oh, Rosemary, I'm so sorry."

"It was a tremendous shock. I feel so dreadful, being away . . ."

"I feel guilty too. I should have gone round, but then I got this beastly thing that knocked me out. And I really did think she was getting over it—when I rang she said she just wanted to be on her own."

Rosemary shook her head. "No, there was probably nothing any of us could have done. It's just that, well, she is—was—family. You know how it is."

"Does your mother know?"

"No, I thought I'd leave it until we knew more about things. It will be such a shock and Elsie says she's really been quite ill."

"Yes, it was quite a virulent bug. How did you hear?"

"Dr. Porter phoned me, because he knew we were related and they needed a relative to make arrangements and so on. Of course I wasn't there, so he told Jack, who phoned me. It was awful when I got the message—I couldn't believe it. Eva's always been so lively, so active." She bit her lip to stop the tears. "She was always so special to me."

"I know."

Rosemary sighed. "And I've had such a marvelous week. Oxford was wonderful, and Stratford, and it was so nice doing things with Jilly—it makes it feel worse somehow . . ."

"Nonsense," I said. "No matter what has happened, Eva would have been so pleased you've had a lovely time. She was all for people enjoying themselves. Now, I'm going to put the kettle on and you must tell me all about it."

The news of Eva's death was a surprise and shock to a great many people. When I felt able to go to Brunswick Lodge a few days later it was still the main topic of conversation.

"Such a terrible thing to have happened," Alison Shelby was saying when I arrived. "And lying there like that for all those days. It doesn't bear thinking about." She became aware of my presence. "Of course, you were such a great friend—you must feel dreadful about it."

"Yes," I said briefly. "It was a great shock."

"And poor Rosemary—*she* was away, wasn't she? What a thing to come back to."

I didn't reply and she went on, "Donald was really upset—well, they'd become quite close, if you know what I mean. At least, that's what I've been given to believe. And he was away too. Imagine what *he* must be feeling."

"I think he was away on business," Maureen Philips said. "Not just on holiday."

"We don't know yet what caused poor Eva's death," Matthew Paisley broke in. "It's a bit soon to be apportioning the guilt."

"Oh no," Alison said hastily, "I never meant—"

"So we don't know if anyone could have done anything to help her," Matthew persisted.

"No, of course not. I just thought . . ."

"I tried to ring her," Maureen said. "I thought she might know when Donald would be back. I needed to tell him about a committee meeting. But there was no reply. That was on the Wednesday. Do you think that she was, you know, *then*?"

"Oh dear," Alison clasped her hands together in a dramatic gesture. "How *awful*! When did the cleaner find her?"

"I think she goes in on a Friday," Maureen said. "I seem to remember Eva saying it was sometimes awkward because she always liked to do any writing she had on Fridays and it was a bit difficult with Mrs. Mac hoovering all round her."

"So if you phoned on the Wednesday, then she might—"

"We won't know anything until after the postmortem," Matthew said abruptly. "I think we should stop all this speculation." He looked at me. "It must be very distressing for her close friends and family."

"Oh no—I wouldn't dream . . ." Maureen said hastily. "I'm sorry, Sheila."

"I think Matthew is right," I said. "We won't know what actually happened until Dr. Porter informs the family."

"They've got the postmortem results," Rosemary said.

"Was it this virus thing?" I asked.

"In a way. It was the diabetes, really. She died because she didn't take her insulin."

"But she was always so good about that."

"Dr. Porter thinks she was feeling so ill with that wretched virus that she simply forgot," Rosemary said. "And then, of course, she was dehydrated anyway. There's something called diabetic acidosis that can be caused by gastritis. Apparently it's the fever and vomiting—you don't take your insulin. It's all very complicated—I don't understand the half of it. But so awful—if I'd been here I'd have been able to see to her. It need never have happened . . ." Her voice trailed away.

"It's not your *fault*," I said vehemently. "No one could have foreseen it. I feel guilty too. I should have followed up my phone call. I might have been in time to save her. I feel terrible about it. But it's happened and it's dreadful and there's nothing we can do about it now."

We were both silent for a moment, then Rosemary said, "Of course, I've had to tell Mother."

"Oh dear. How did she take it?"

"Surprisingly well, really, I thought. She was very upset."

"I suppose," I said thoughtfully, "that if you're really old, then death isn't such a surprise. I mean, you're used—in a way—to your friends dying . . ."

"She talked a lot about Alan and how devoted he and Eva were."

"How about Daniel?"

"Absolutely devastated, poor boy. Losing Eva so soon after Alan. I know he didn't see a lot of them—he'd got his own life—but they were all very close. Thank goodness he's got Patrick."

"Yes, he struck me as being someone who'd be good in a crisis."

"They're coming down for the funeral—we can arrange that now. Well, I said I'd do everything. I think Eva would want it down here. Mother and I thought she'd like to be buried near her parents; Alan was cremated, of course. Daniel said he'd leave it all to me and Patrick seemed to think it was the best plan."

"Is there anything I can do?"

"Not really. It's all in hand now and I've seen the vicar of St. Mary's. Such a nice man, very helpful. There's a spot in the graveyard quite close to her parents' graves."

"She'd like that."

"Yes. Oh, Sheila," Rosemary burst out, "all this suddenly makes it real. Somehow it wasn't before . . ."

"I know. Just at first you can abstract your mind in a way, but there comes a moment when it hits you and you know it's really happened and nothing's ever going to change that.

Chapter Seven

St. Mary's is a small church a few miles outside Taviscombe. Originally built in the Middle Ages, it was thoroughly restored in the Victorian Gothic style, which nowadays has a sort of nostalgic charm. The original graveyard immediately surrounding the church is full of leaning headstones whose inscriptions have been mostly obliterated, except where some earnest ancestor-seeker has scraped away the lichen in search of information which will complete the family tree.

The field next to the original burial ground was taken in a hundred years ago and this so-called "new" graveyard houses the remains of the more recent inhabitants of the nearby villages and also others who were technically of that parish—both Peter and my mother lie there—and had expressed a wish to be

buried there instead of in the large Taviscombe ceme-
tery. It too has its lichen-covered stones, since the pure,
damp air promotes such green coverings, but there
are also more modern, and to some, less attractive
memorials. As I stood by Eva's grave, I could see what
might be described as an art deco memorial, angu-
larly shaped with eye-catching green and black deco-
rations. The subject of many furious objections long
ago, when it was first put up, over the years (and after
several laudatory articles about it in *Country Life* and
other journals), it has acquired a sort of respectable
fame and now people come from some distance to
see it. And I remembered how Rosemary, Eva and I,
with the enthusiasm of youth, praised it as an exam-
ple of modern art, in the face of the horrified opposition of our parents.

Eva would have a traditional stone, like that of
her parents nearby. Daniel had left the arrangements
to Rosemary and had only come down to Taviscombe
a few days before the funeral. I saw him, his arm
supporting Mrs. Dudley, as the family came into the
church. There was a good congregation; Eva had made
many friends in the short time since her return. As
well as the family and a few friends from the old
days, there was a large group from Brunswick Lodge,
including Donald. I hadn't seen him since Eva died.
He was sitting behind me in the church so I wasn't
able to see him there, but here, outside, he looked hag-
gard and weary. He'd been away and it must have
hit him hard to come back to such news.

By the graveside the vicar pronounced the traditional, solemn words, earth was sprinkled and we all turned away, some more slowly than others, and made our way to our cars and the buffet lunch that Rosemary had arranged nearby. Here, in the warmth and the comfort of the hotel, people relaxed, with reminiscences and more general chat and there was, as there so often is, a sort of party atmosphere ("What Eva would have wanted").

"I think it all went off all right," Rosemary said as she paused beside me for a moment with a plate of food for her mother. "Do you think?"

"Perfectly," I said. "It was a lovely service and so many people came."

"It was a big responsibility. Daniel's been in a very bad way and I wasn't sure what he wanted. Fortunately Patrick was marvelous and was able to get through to him when none of us could."

"Where's Patrick now?"

"Over there, helping Jilly with Mother, bless him."

I looked across at the little group—Mrs. Dudley ensconced on a sofa with Jilly beside her and Patrick, bending toward her, talking earnestly. There was no sign of Daniel.

I looked inquiringly at Rosemary.

"He went outside for a bit," she said. "I think he found all this a bit much."

"How long are they staying?"

"I don't know. We're sort of living from day to

day. They're staying with us, of course. Daniel won't go near the cottage." She sighed. "Well, I'd better get this food to Mother—she was very scornful about the buffet because there wasn't a whole ham."

I didn't feel in the least like eating, but, for the look of the thing, I went over to the buffet. In spite of the lack of a ham there was a wide variety of food and I took various things at random and a glass of wine, which I felt was something I really needed.

"Quite a good turnout." Matthew Paisley, with a group from Brunswick Lodge, came up beside me.

"Yes," I said, "I'm glad the church was so full."

"We're going to miss her," he continued. "She was always so helpful about doing things."

"Such a lovely person," Alison Shelby broke in, "and really quite distinguished in her own right—I read some of her articles; they were very good. She fitted in so well."

"Well, she did come from here," Matthew said reprovingly, "and her family have lived round here for years."

"Oh yes, of course—I didn't mean . . . So what will happen to her cottage?" Alison asked.

"I don't know," I said. "I don't imagine Daniel will want to keep it."

"Daniel?"

"Her son."

"*Really?* I didn't know she had a son."

"He lives in London."

"Fancy that." She looked round the room. "Which is he?"

"I don't think he's here just at the moment," I said.

"What a pity—I'd like to have told him how sorry we all are."

"I'm sure he knows that."

"I do feel so sorry for poor Donald," Maureen Philips broke in. She leaned confidently toward me. "He was quite attached, wasn't he? To Eva, I mean. Well, we all noticed and wondered if something might come of it." She looked at me expectantly.

"I really don't know," I said. "Do excuse me." I gestured with my glass. "I really must find somewhere to sit down with this lot."

I was making my way toward an empty table—I really didn't feel like talking to anyone—when I saw that Mrs. Dudley was waving me over to join her. I put my plate down on the table beside her and she regarded it critically.

"I'm glad to see you didn't have any slices of that ham," she said. "It gets so dry if it's not cut freshly every time."

I nodded agreement. Obviously the subject of the ham was her defense to hide her actual feelings. I looked at Rosemary and she smiled faintly.

"How is Daniel?" I asked Patrick.

He shrugged. "Not good. He went outside for a bit. It hasn't really sunk in yet. So soon after his father. He'll be all right—he's pretty tough and determined under that casual exterior."

"He's very lucky to have you to help him through things."

"We've been together for a long time now. And we work together pretty well."

I glanced at Mrs. Dudley, uncertain what she felt about this particular relationship.

She was smiling approvingly at Patrick. "It takes a very special kind of person to deal with someone like Daniel and he's very lucky to have you." She turned to me. "Do you know, he arranged every detail of that service."

"Well, Rosemary had done most of it," Patrick said. "I just filled in a few things that Daniel wanted."

"It was beautifully done," I said. "I'm sure it's exactly what Eva would have wanted." I paused for a moment then asked, "How long will you be staying? Do you have to get back to London?"

"Oh no," Mrs. Dudley broke in, "there's no question of that. No question at all."

"I think I can persuade him to stay for a while," Patrick said. "I've canceled all his commitments in London—there's nothing he needs to get back for."

Mrs. Dudley nodded. "Exactly." She turned to him. "I still think you both should come and stay with me. Rosemary leads such a busy life." (Rosemary nobly refrained from reacting to this well-worn phrase.) "I'm sure you'd be much more comfortable with me—Elsie has practically nothing to do all day." I tried not to catch Rosemary's eye. "And she will enjoy looking after you."

Patrick smiled. " It's so good of you," he said, "and, of course, we'd love to come, but I think that while

Daniel is fairly settled at the moment, we'd better leave things as they are."

Rosemary got up. "I'd better go and have a word with the hotel staff," she said.

I got to my feet too. "And I must go and talk to the Brunswick Lodge people. Do give my love to Daniel and tell him I'd like to see him sometime while he's here."

When we were out of earshot I said to Rosemary, "What was all that about?"

She laughed. "Oh you know Mother—she can't bear not to be the center of attention. Of course she's really fond of Daniel but she knew perfectly well that they wouldn't go and stay with her. But, this way, she gained brownie points for having made the offer without the trouble of having it accepted."

To everyone's surprise, Daniel decided to move into Eva's cottage.

"We were absolutely flabbergasted," Rosemary said when she called round a few days later. "After how he was reacting to things right up to the funeral."

"Was it his decision?" I asked tentatively. "I mean, did Patrick suggest it?"

"No. He just said, out of the blue, that that was what he wanted to do. I think Patrick was as surprised as we were."

"Does he have any idea why?"

"He thinks it's Daniel's way of facing up to things."

"Good, if he can, but rather drastic."

"I think he does make decisions like that—quite suddenly. Anyway, I've had the heating put on and got some food in. Mrs. Mac will look in and do anything they want. It might help Daniel decide what to do with things down here."

"He might want to keep the cottage," I suggested.

Rosemary shook her head. "I honestly don't know. He's an odd person, not in the least like Alan or Eva. He seems to live in a world of his own."

"But surely he has to be practical in his job. All the technical things about food and cooking and so forth."

"Oh yes, he's very professional and focused about that—well that *is* like Alan, like Eva too for that matter. But in his actual life he tends to plunge about and relies on Patrick to make things work for him."

"Do they have other friends?"

"No, apparently not. Daniel's always been a loner—I don't even know how he met Patrick."

"I was interested to see how your mother reacted to that relationship."

"Oh, Mother's a pragmatist. If it works, and she happens to take to the people involved, she's all for it. Do you remember Dora Makepeace and Lily Foster; they lived in that big house on West Hill that belonged to Dora's family?"

"Oh yes. Dora and 'my friend that I live with.' And I remember that your mother was very thick with them."

"Exactly. It worked and it suited her to be friendly with them—they were a wonderful source of gossip.

And, to be fair, she's very fond of Daniel and she can see how hopeless he would be without Patrick."

"Well, it would be good if they could, between them, sort out those papers. I don't think Eva ever got down to actually doing anything about them."

"She never really wanted to—because of Alan." Rosemary sighed. "And then she got sidetracked."

I was silent for a moment. "I suppose you mean Donald?" She nodded. "I think he made her happy," I said tentatively.

"Yes, you're quite right. I shouldn't have begrudged her that." She was silent for a moment.

"I was put out in a way. I'd sort of planned in my mind how she was going to lead her life now that she was down here. What things we'd all do together, that kind of thing, and how we'd support her now that Alan had died. I didn't give her credit for being a person in her own right, able to make her own decisions."

"You wanted to help."

"Yes, but in a selfish way. I do regret it now."

I didn't see anything of Daniel and Patrick for a while. I had a couple of difficult reviews to do and had to concentrate on them, not helped by Tris suddenly getting lice, which resisted all chemical forms of destruction but had to be tracked down with a fine comb and disposed of one by one. While all this was going on, Foss, resentful at the extra attention Tris was getting, was particularly tiresome, rejecting previously favorite foods and only accepting freshly cooked fish or chicken. He took to weaving round my feet in the kitchen, once tripping me over so that I lurched into the worktop, heavily bruising my right hand, making the use of my computer very difficult.

"I can't see why you make such a fuss of them," Anthea said when I was complaining about the complications of my life. "After all, they're only animals."

Over the years I've learned to ignore most of Anthea's tiresome remarks.

"Oh well, I'm managing, but it's all taking longer than I expected so I'm afraid I won't be able to come to the committee meeting on Tuesday. I'm sorry."

"Really, Sheila," Anthea said crossly, "it's only for an hour at the most, and you know how important it is to settle things about having that electrical work done. Derek is being so difficult about the money. I've told him, time and time again, how dangerous it would be to leave things as they are."

Since the electrical work that Anthea referred to consisted of putting a couple of extra points in the kitchen for certain gadgets that Anthea has set her heart on, I was inclined to side with Derek this time. And, as for the committee meeting only lasting an hour—well, it would be the first time in the history of Brunswick Lodge if this happened. Knowing that it was always impossible to argue rationally with Anthea, I repeated my apology and retreated into the office where I found Alison Shelby, who was sorting out some leaflets. She greeted me eagerly.

"Oh, Sheila, you can tell me—how is that poor boy?"

"Poor boy?" I echoed.

"Eva's son—Daniel. I hadn't realized that he was really quite famous. Maureen was telling me all about him. Writing in the Sunday papers, and on television too! What a gifted family—all three of them. That is— is Daniel the only child?"

"Yes," I said repressively. "He is." I certainly didn't feel like discussing Daniel with anyone, let alone Alison. "However," I went on, "I think he just wants to be left alone to come to terms with things."

"*So* tragic. To lose both parents like that."

I nodded.

"And going to live in that cottage—so brave. Will he be staying on there, do you think? Of course, living in London as he does, he might want to keep it as a holiday cottage. What do you think?"

"I'm afraid I don't know."

"I was saying to Maurice, the other day, what a job it would be to clear it. I mean, Eva had more or less just come down here with all her stuff from London— downsizing, isn't that what they call it?—and Maureen said there were a lot of papers and things of her husband's. All to be sorted out."

"No doubt he will make his own arrangements," I said shortly.

But, as always, there was no way of stopping Alison.

"Of course, he's got that nice friend of his to help

him. A pleasant young man, very quiet, not much to say for himself, but I'm sure he's a great help. Maureen said he more or less organized the funeral. But at such a time! And a dreadful shock. I mean, who would have thought poor Eva would go, quite suddenly like that? And a postmortem, too, terribly upsetting for everyone. I was so sorry for Rosemary, losing a relation like that."

"Do you need any help with those leaflets?" I asked.

"Oh no, they're the ones about the recital. I was just seeing how many I needed to take—I promised Anthea that I'd hand them out at the next WI meeting."

"Oh, right, I'll leave you to it, then." I said, edging through the door.

It was obvious that Daniel (now they knew that he was a television personality) was exciting quite an interest among the members of Brunswick Lodge, but I was sure that Patrick was more than capable of protecting him from their attentions.

Chapter Eight

I was just coming out of the chemist when I ran straight into Donald Webster. Flustered, I muttered some sort of apology and he looked concerned.

"Are you all right?" he asked. "You look a bit put out."

"Oh, I'm all right," I said, "but it's chaos in there. I've been trying to collect my prescription. It was silly to come at this time of day, of course—it's always crowded, an endless queue and, when you do reach the counter, they're so busy it takes forever for them to find anything. I was there for ages. Then," I went on, "when I finally got the prescription it turned out to be the wrong one—I'd almost got to the door when I realized. So I had to go back again . . . well, I *am* a bit put out!"

He smiled. "You poor thing. What you need is a

coffee." I hesitated for a moment and he said, "Come on; a coffee and a nice sit-down."

"Oh, yes, please," I said gratefully, "that is exactly what I need."

Amazingly, the Buttery wasn't as crowded as usual and we managed to get a table out of the way at the back.

"Better?" he asked when I'd sipped my coffee.

"Much better." I could see how this sort of sympathetic attention—even over such a trivial occurrence—could be very attractive. "I was hoping to have a word with you," I said.

"And I wanted to have a word with you."

We were both silent, then he said, "You go first."

"It's just to say how sorry I am—it must have been such a terrible shock to get the news like that when you got back."

"It was pretty devastating. That's one of the reasons I wanted to speak to you. I still only have the bare fact of . . . her . . . of Eva's death. I don't really know what happened."

"That's awful," I said. "I assumed someone must have told you."

"I hadn't seen anyone," he said, "and, although I went to the service, I didn't feel I could face seeing people afterward."

So I told him all the circumstances, trying to soften things as best I could.

When I'd finished, he turned his head away so that I couldn't see his face. Then he said, "Thank you,

Sheila. I'm afraid it must have been painful for you to go over it all like that."

I shook my head. "I've gone over it all in my head almost every day since she died," I said. "Feeling so guilty that I didn't try again when there was no reply. I might have been able to save her. Instead . . ."

"No," he said swiftly, "you mustn't feel like that. There's no way you could have known."

"It's the 'if only' thing. Poor Rosemary feels the same. If only she hadn't gone away that week . . ."

"If only I hadn't had to go away," he said. "I feel it too." He paused. "It's the awful thought of her lying there when something could have been done."

"Accidental death, they said, and of course it was. But it's knowing that it could have so *easily* been prevented that really hurts. It was so . . . so unnecessary!"

"Yes."

"Just a combination of circumstances—that's what I keep telling myself. But it doesn't help."

"I don't think anything will really help," he said. "Not for a long time, anyway."

"She'll be missed by a lot of people."

"Eva was the sort of person everyone warms to—she was such a warm person herself."

"She always did make friends easily. People felt comfortable with her."

"You and Rosemary were lucky—you knew her all those years ago."

"It's like school friends," I said thoughtfully. "You

either lose touch completely or are friends for life. There's no real reason for it. I remember, after one Old Girls' reunion I said to Rosemary about one of the people there, 'She's really such a nice person. Why did we hate her?' Very odd."

"I don't think I'd recognize a single person I was at school with," Donald said. "But then that was in another country and I've moved around quite a bit since then. I envy you people; you have the sort of stability I'm only just beginning to need." He paused for a moment and then said, "How about Eva? Did she come to want that sort of stability? Did she resent Alan being away so much? I never got around to asking her."

"I'm sure she accepted Alan's lifestyle when she married him. Perhaps, after Daniel was born, she may have wished he'd been there a bit more, but she'd never have wanted to change him. She knew that was the life he'd chosen—absence, danger, the lot—and she understood."

"A rare quality."

"Yes. And I believe it was a happy marriage."

"What about Daniel? Do you think it made a difference to him?"

"I don't really know Daniel very well. He's very eccentric, I suppose, but I have the feeling that's *him* if you know what I mean. In the genes, perhaps. He admired his father, probably loved him, and he and Eva were devoted but apart; they loved each other but didn't feel the need to be together all the time. At least, that's how I see it."

"She never really talked about him to me, just the occasional, casual reference. I suppose it might have struck me as odd—most mothers are full of their children's doings—but, somehow it didn't occur to me to wonder about it. Of course," he went on, "it might have cropped up quite soon."

I looked at him inquiringly. "Oh?"

"I asked Eva to marry me and I expect the subject of how Daniel would take it would have been mentioned sometime."

So that had been the serious thing that Donald wanted to talk to her about that day at Brunswick Lodge. Somehow I wasn't really surprised.

"I see," I said. "And did she accept you? I'm sorry, I shouldn't ask you that."

"No, it's all right. I'd like you and Rosemary to know. I don't know if she'd been expecting it or not. We'd been good friends and just good friends, but I felt we'd become really close to each other and I think women see these things more clearly than men do."

"True."

He smiled. "Anyway, she said she needed time to think about it. I felt it wasn't a refusal, but simply what she needed to do. That's what I hoped, anyway. As you know, I had to go away for a while and she said she'd give me an answer when I got back . . ." His voice broke on the last word.

"And when you got back—I'm so very sorry. So much worse for you than I realized."

"Yes. Another if only," he said sadly. "I persuaded myself she would have married me. Not then, too soon after Alan's death, but sometime, when we'd really got to know each other."

"I don't know if it helps," I said, "but I think you're right. You suited each other and enjoyed each other's company. That's no bad basis for marriage."

"Well, we'll never know now."

"Will you stay in Taviscombe?" I asked. "Now, I mean."

"I don't know—it's all too soon to decide. I suppose I've built up a sort of life here, even if . . ."

"You've made a lot of friends. People want to involve you in things—if that's enough."

"I hope you and Rosemary will count yourselves among my friends," he said. "That is, if Rosemary will forgive me for having monopolized Eva."

"I think so. It might take a little time."

He smiled. "Oh well, there's always Mrs. Dudley."

When I told Rosemary that Donald had asked Eva to marry him, she said, "There, I knew that would happen!"

"Would it have been such a bad thing? It wouldn't have been right away, and I think it would have made Eva happy."

"Oh, I don't know," she said impatiently. "It might have worked out. I'm sorry I was so dog-in-the-manger-ish. It was selfish of me. I can see that now. It's just that we know so little about him."

"I think he was genuinely fond of her and she really enjoyed being with him. You must admit, she brightened up considerably when he came into her life. To be honest, I don't think Eva was cut out to be a widow—some people just aren't."

"You seem to have managed all right."

"That's different. Peter and I were together all the time, all those years. He was part of my life—that's why I could never think of anyone else. Eva and Alan were quite different—in a way they led separate lives, even though they were married. And Donald was very much her sort of person—he'd lived in the kind of world she knew about; they had a lot in common."

"I suppose so."

"It was awful," I said. "He didn't know anything except the actual fact that she'd died. He was absolutely shattered when I told him how it was."

"Poor man." Her voice softened. "That must have been terrible for him."

"Like us, he feels guilty that he wasn't there for her. He really did love her."

"And you're right," Rosemary said. "He did seem to make her happy—she was much more like the old Eva when he was around." She was thoughtful for a moment. "What's he going to do? Is he going to stay here?"

"I don't think he knows what he wants to do. Like I said, he hasn't had a chance to come to terms with what's happened."

"What about Daniel?" Rosemary asked. "Had Eva told him she might be marrying Donald?"

"I don't think so. He said that they hadn't got around to talking about that. How do you think Daniel would have felt?"

"Goodness only knows—Daniel seems to live in a world of his own most of the time. I don't think he'd have minded—who knows!"

"Will you tell him?"

"I don't know. What do you think?"

"I think, perhaps, he ought to know."

"I'll see how it goes. He and Patrick are coming to lunch tomorrow—though that may not be the best time—Mother suggested it and I think she was right. I know he's not a great one for family, but I do feel he ought to know we're around if he wants us. Actually, he and Mother get on rather well—he seems to connect with her in a way most young people can't."

"They're both individuals," I said. "Perhaps that's the reason."

"Well, whatever it is, I'm grateful for it."

"And what about your mother? Will you tell *her* about Donald?"

"Since it's something she's been predicting more or less since he came here, I'm sure she'll be telling me!"

Daniel and Patrick seemed to have settled into Eva's cottage and there was no talk of them going back to London. They weren't seen much in Taviscombe—there were occasional sightings of Patrick in the farm shop and the local delicatessen, but that was all.

"Such a shame they don't take *part* in things a bit more," Anthea said. "I'm sure we'd all be fascinated to hear a talk about London restaurants from Daniel."

"For goodness' sake, Anthea!" I said in exasperation. "The poor boy has only just lost his mother! Just leave him in peace."

"Oh, I wouldn't dream of asking him to do anything now. But I do feel it might help him to get out into the world again. It can't be good for him to be shut away out there with that friend of his."

I could see that Anthea was dying to extract more information about Daniel and Patrick so I changed the subject to the continuing battle between her and Derek about "improvements" to the kitchen in the hope that, if she did approach them, Patrick would be quite capable of fending her off.

I thought about them a great deal over the next week or so, there in their own little world, so I was surprised to get a phone call from Patrick, inviting me to dinner the next day.

"Of course I accepted," I said to Rosemary. "Will you be there?"

"Yes, Jack and I will both go. Jack was a bit reluctant; he says he never knows what to say to Daniel. But he can talk to Patrick—*he's* always easy to talk to."

"Who else will be there?" I asked.

"Oh, just us, just family."

"I'm honored! I must say, I was surprised to hear from them."

"Well, Daniel knows you go way back with Eva

too. Anyway, I expect Daniel wants to talk to you
about those Victorian novelists. You both seemed to
have a lot to say last time you met."

I thought it would be upsetting, going to the cottage, but somehow it didn't feel the same as it had
when Eva was there. It's not that there were any actual
alterations, but the furniture had been rearranged and
there were quite a few magazines lying around and
some very beautiful flower arrangements. It seemed
that Patrick (I was sure that it was Patrick) had managed to recreate Daniel's world around him and I felt
that was probably something he did whenever they
were away from home. It was Patrick, too, who had
done the cooking. Nothing fancy. Beautifully cooked
roast lamb and vegetables, all of the highest quality
and all tasting perfectly of themselves, followed by a
superb lemon tart.

Daniel and I did have a short chat about George
Eliot (who we both disliked) but the conversation
was general. Daniel said that he was going to stay at
the cottage for a while.

Patrick said Daniel had been working too hard
and needed a break anyway. And, of course, there
would be quite a lot to do about things—deciding
about the cottage and so forth. Also, Daniel said, they
ought to go through his father's papers, to prepare
them for publication—he knew that's what his mother had been going to do and Patrick was good at
that sort of thing. Jack asked if Daniel was going to
keep the cottage and Daniel said he hadn't decided,
but if he did sell, it wouldn't be to the neighboring

farmer who'd been badgering him with offers, and Jack said he'd be happy to help with contracts and things if Daniel decided he did want to sell. It was a surprisingly ordinary evening and not at all what I'd been expecting.

I said as much to Rosemary when she phoned the next day.

"That's Patrick. He knows exactly how much 'ordinary' life Daniel needs and provides it when necessary. He saw how good he was with Mother and I suppose he decided that what Daniel needed just now was family."

"I'm surprised Daniel wanted to stay at the cottage, especially considering how he was just after Eva died."

"That was Patrick too. He apparently thought that Daniel needed a project—his father's papers. A real break from his usual life."

"He really is an amazing person—Patrick, I mean. He must be very devoted to Daniel."

"Yes. I suppose so."

"You don't seem very certain."

"I really don't know what to make of him. *Is* he devoted, or is he just a sort of super-secretary? It isn't that he's a cold person, but there's a kind of cool decisiveness about him."

"They seem to get on remarkably well—lots of jokes and lively chat."

"Yes, they're very much on the same wavelength, and completely at ease with each other—partners in every sense of the word, yes, and Patrick is devoted, in the sense that I'm sure he'd do anything *for* Daniel, but there's a certain reserve. I can't explain, and, goodness knows, I'm so grateful that he's there—I can't imagine what Daniel would do without him, especially now."

Chapter Nine

It was only a few days after the dinner party that I came across Daniel again. I'd gone down to look across the Bristol Channel, as I quite often do after shopping, when I saw him leaning on the sea wall. It was dull and overcast, the sort of day when the sea and sky merge into one uniform gray and the water is hardly moving, and even the most enthusiastic walker hasn't been tempted to venture out. The gloomy day and the solitary figure provided such a melancholy picture that I was uncertain whether or not to approach. However, he lifted his head and had obviously seen me so I felt I could join him.

"You made such a perfect picture, all alone, leaning on the sea wall on this miserable day," I said, "that I hardly liked to spoil it."

He smiled. "I didn't actually arrange myself in

this position for effect," he said. "I just wanted to think."

"I've interrupted you—I'm sorry."

"No, it's all right; I've had my think."

"And did you come to any conclusion?" I asked.

"As a matter of fact I did."

"That's good."

He smiled again. "I've decided I'd like to stay here for a while. Quite a while, actually."

"To sort through your father's papers?"

"That as well, but it's more than that." He paused and looked out to sea again. "Down here I suddenly felt free. My life has become so busy, so *convoluted* that I've become overwhelmed by it. Down here," he repeated and paused again. ". . . down here I could breathe again and not have to keep looking ahead. I could just *be*."

"That would be good."

"Especially on a day like this when there's no one else about; just me and the sea." He gestured toward it. "Just look at it—isn't it perfect?"

"A bit melancholy today," I said.

"But it's *real*! I think that's what I've missed. I haven't been living in the real world."

"I suppose you haven't."

He took a couple of deep breaths. "There, you see—fresh air, wonderful!"

I laughed. "There's plenty of that down here."

Daniel smiled. "Yes, well, I get up early in the morning now—at first light—and go out running. It's amazing—everywhere is empty. It's a terrific feeling. Botox for the spirit—gets rid of all the wrinkles in your mind and leaves it clear and smooth." He gestured again. "Like the sea today."

"The sea isn't always as smooth as this," I said. "It can be very rough sometimes."

"Oh, I know that. Do you ever listen to the shipping forecast on the radio? I love it. Viking, North Utsire, South Utsire, Dogger, Fisher, German Bight, FitzRoy, Lundy, Rockall, Malin, Fair Isle, Faeroes." He chanted the names. "Fantastic—it's hypnotic. And the weather—southwesterly 7 to severe gale 9, rough or high, moderate to poor. Yes, the sea isn't always calm!"

He stopped suddenly. "I suppose you think I'm mad."

I shook my head. "No, just excited because you've discovered something new. It's good. And, yes, I do listen to the shipping forecast—when I wake early. I love it too." I smiled. "For what it's worth, I think you've made the right choice. I think you do need a break from your other lifestyle. I think Eva would approve."

He nodded. "When she said she was coming back here after my father died, I thought she was making a mistake. Her life's always been in London—most of her friends are there. But I can see now that she wanted to—how do they put it?—get back to her roots. She was even doing research into the family on the Internet, making a family tree—her side and my father's. I don't think she'd got very far, but I'd rather like to go on with it."

"Good for you."

"I'm going to talk to Cousin Doris about it—her memory must go back a long way."

Identifying, with some difficulty, Mrs. Dudley, I agreed that she would certainly be a useful source.

"I like her. She's a bit of a dragon, but we get on."

"She's a great one for family," I said. "She approves of you."

"Good."

"And Patrick approves of all this?" I asked. "Staying down here, I mean."

"He's all for it. Actually, he's been on at me for ages to take a break."

"He won't find it too boring after London?"

"Oh, he'll find something to do. Patrick could find something in the middle of the Kalahari Desert. Though, as a matter of fact, he's a country boy—came from some remote part of Ireland. I don't know where." He smiled. "Somehow, one doesn't ask Patrick about personal things."

"Not even you?"

"No. That's why we get on so well together—we respect each other's space."

"Well, I'm glad he'll feel happy here."

There was a silence, though a comfortable one, as we both stared out at the sea and the faint, almost indistinguishable outline of the Welsh coast. Emboldened by this I asked, "Did your mother ever talk to you about Donald Webster?"

He turned his head sharply and looked at me.

"No—well, not *talked*. She mentioned him occasionally in passing. Why?"

"He asked her to marry him."

"Oh."

"He was just about to go away for a while and
she said she'd give him her answer when he came
back. But then . . ."

"She died."

"Yes."

"And do you think she would have?"

"I don't know. I believe she wanted time to think
about it. It was too soon after Alan's death, but I
think she might have agreed eventually. They got on
well together, enjoyed each other's company—but
as good friends, nothing more."

"I see."

"She'd made a lot of friends down here and there
was Rosemary, of course, but I think she was lonely.
Well, missing a special person—one does."

He was silent for quite a while and I began to
regret bringing the matter up and wishing that Rosemary, who, after all, was a more suitable person, had
found the opportunity to tell him.

"Thank you for telling me."

"I hope I haven't upset you."

"No, I needed to know." He paused. "It's just that
it takes a bit of thinking about. I wish I could have
talked to her about it . . ."

"She would have told you if she'd decided."

"Yes, of course. But I suppose we led such separate

lives. I've only just realized that. There are a great many things we didn't tell each other and now it's too late. That's sad."

"I think we all feel that, or something like it, when someone close to us dies. But that's just something you have to accept and get on with your life."

"You're right, of course. That's what Patrick says."

"Patrick is a very wise person," I said.

"Yes he is. I don't think I could carry on without him."

"So Daniel's going to stay on at the cottage," I said to Rosemary as we were sorting some books for the book sale at Brunswick Lodge. "I saw him down by the harbor. He was in a strange sort of mood—really excited, more animated than I've ever seen him; you know how laid-back he usually is. Talking about things being *real* down here."

"Yes. I must say I was surprised when he told me, but I'm sure it's a good thing. He was very wound up when he came down for the funeral, and, although he's still sort of wound up, it's in a different way."

"I suppose the life he was leading in London was very artificial in some ways and quite a strain."

"I know Patrick's pleased they're staying. I think he'd got quite worried about things. He seems to like being down here. He's planning to begin looking through Alan's papers—I don't believe Daniel's up to that yet, but Patrick thinks that if he gets started, Daniel might become interested."

"Good for him."

"Mother's delighted, of course. Daniel's been spending quite a lot of time with her. Apparently Eva had started looking up the family on the Internet, Alan's family too—all that genealogy stuff—and Daniel's going on with it."

"Yes, he told me he was going to ask your mother what she remembered about her generation. It was quite a shock when he referred to her as Cousin Doris!"

"I know. That was Mother's idea; it makes her feel rather grand and Victorian. Anyway, she's thrilled to have someone who actually *wants* to hear about all the relations and off-relations. And Elsie loves having someone who appreciates her cakes and scones. All wonderful for Mother, wonderful for me, too—she's in a permanently good mood nowadays."

"Good for Daniel. I must say it's not a thing I would ever have thought of him doing. But that's not the only thing. Did you know that he now gets up at first light and goes running!"

"Good heavens—that's the last thing I'd have thought of!"

Alison Shelby, who'd been hovering nearby, came up with some books in her hand.

"Sorry to interrupt," she said, "but I wondered if these would be all right for the sale. I've been having a bit of a turn-out and, really, we do seem to have a lot of books nobody ever reads."

She handed them over and I looked at them with some curiosity, wondering what sort of books the Shelbys read. There was a guide to Hadrian's Wall,

The Letters of Queen Victoria, Tennyson's poems, *Little Women* and *Good Wives*.

"Actually, they belonged to Maurice's mother," she said. "Not the sort of things we would care for. Well, Maurice only reads those stuffy old law books and things about the First World War, and really I don't have time for reading. I like a good magazine, but books take up so much time, don't they?"

"Didn't your daughters read *Little Women*?" I asked.

"Oh no," she said quickly, "that's very old-fashioned, isn't it? Nobody reads that sort of thing nowadays, do they?"

I was careful not to look at Rosemary. We are both devoted to Louisa Alcott and renew our acquaintance with the March family quite frequently.

"Well, thank you. They can go into the sale," I said. "I'm sure someone would like them."

"Oh good. It seemed a shame to throw them out."

I was delighted to get an invitation to tea with Mrs. Dudley with the information that Daniel would be there. I was eager to see her in the role of Cousin Doris. When she let me in, Elsie whispered, "*Such* a difference since Mr. Daniel's been here. Quite cheered her up!"

Certainly the atmosphere was much livelier than usual. Instead of sitting immovably in her chair by the fire, Mrs. Dudley was seated at the large table in the center of the room, which was covered with albums. Daniel was sitting beside her sorting through a large number of loose photographs scattered around them. When she saw me, Mrs. Dudley raised her head and called me over.

"Ah, Sheila, this will interest you—a photograph of your parents, taken, I believe, in the 1930s at a garden party we all went to at the castle."

The castle was Dunster Castle, now in the hands of the National Trust to Mrs. Dudley's profound regret (*"Another* beautiful home gone!") since, in her youth, it had been the scene of many eagerly sought after social occasions.

I looked at the photograph, sepia with age, so much a part of history now that it seemed almost impossible that anyone in that group, caught forever in time, should still be alive today.

"How interesting," I said. "I don't think I've ever seen that one."

"I remember that hat your mother was wearing," Mrs. Dudley said. "It didn't have a brim—we all thought that very new and daring. Your mother," she continued, "was always very *fashionable*." And I could catch quite clearly the note of disapproval echoing across the years.

Daniel looked up and gave me a quick smile. "Isn't it fascinating?" he said. "Cousin Doris has a wonderful collection of photographs."

"They should all be in albums," Mrs. Dudley said. "I've spoken to Rosemary about it several times. Loose like this, some of them could quite easily get lost. Now, Daniel," she continued, opening one of the albums, "these are the later ones, after the war. This is one of Eva's mother, Lydia. Your grandmother. Now that was taken at a point-to-point somewhere. She had a horse of her own and rode a great deal. She was most disappointed when Eva never showed any sign of wanting her own pony."

I remembered how Eva hated her riding lessons ("I'm scared stiff most of the time and that wretched little pony *knows* and plays me up—he had me off the other day, and Mummy was so disappointed when I wouldn't get straight back on!").

"She hunted too. She led quite a social life and I believe she could have married very well, so it was a great surprise when she decided to marry a colonial. Her family were disappointed, of course, but they made the best of things, even helping him to set up that *business*." The last word was tinged with distaste. "However," she continued, "he did make a success of it and, I believe, made a great deal of money. Not," she added sharply, "that money is everything—not compared with a good family."

"I don't suppose you have anything of *her* parents?" Daniel asked.

"Nothing of her mother, but there is one of her father's father—we share a common great-grandfather—it's in the hall. Sheila, perhaps you will very kindly go and fetch it."

I lifted the framed photograph carefully from its place. It was a formal studio portrait of a man in a frock coat with smoothed-down hair and an air of consequence.

Mrs. Dudley received it with pleasure and handed it to Daniel.

"He looks very important," Daniel said. "What did he do?"

"He was a doctor," Mrs. Dudley said with satisfaction. "I believe he did, on one occasion, attend royalty."

"Sounds very grand." Daniel put the photograph down and picked up one of Eva's mother, Lydia. "She looks very nice, good-looking too—Eva looks very like her. I'll see what I can turn up on the Internet."

Mrs. Dudley was about to express her opinion of the Internet (unfavorable) when Elsie came in and ushered us all into the dining room for tea. Mrs. Dudley was one of the few remaining people I know who still provided a sit-down tea for her visitors and the table was spread with a variety of sandwiches, scones and cakes. I saw with a sinking heart that there was also her best silver tea set, whose heavy teapot I found difficult to manage when Mrs. Dudley, as she always did, required me to pour. However, I did manage it without disgracing myself and the conversation became general.

I was interested to see how Daniel had changed. From being rather remote and formal, he was now lively and enthusiastic, eagerly asking questions about Taviscombe before the war.

"Isn't it extraordinary," he was saying to Mrs. Dudley, "how life has changed in such a relatively short time?"

"And not for the better," was the reply.

It was obvious that Mrs. Dudley was reveling in this attention, something that didn't happen every day, and I was grateful to Daniel for giving her this treat and hoped that this unexpected relationship would continue for the benefit of both of them.

Chapter Ten

"Well, I do think it's been a great success," Anthea said complacently.

I looked over to where the speaker, an elderly man in spectacles, was surrounded by a group of enthusiasts. Though, sadly, the pile of signed copies of his book, the reason for his talk, seemed to be undiminished. "Yes," I agreed. "Local history is always popular."

"It was so splendid that he was able to give Sybil and Pauline a history of their cottage," she went on. "Of course he's made quite a study of that particular period. *Our* house is very much earlier—we have entries in the church records. He was most interested when I told him all about them."

Alison Shelby detached herself from the group and came over.

"Such a good talk! I've always been fascinated by local history. Such a pity Maurice couldn't come today. He's quite an expert, always looking things up on the Internet. I often say he's living in the past, not the present!"

"I'd better go and see how the refreshments are getting on," I said, moving toward the kitchen.

I found Rosemary taking the cling film off plates of small cakes.

"I think we might start taking these in now," she said. "That poor man looked as though he could do with a cup of tea, at least."

"I think he was a bit overwhelmed by the response," I said. "It was a mistake asking if anyone wanted to ask questions. So, of course, after Sybil and Pauline, everyone wanted to know about their own houses."

I helped Rosemary to take in the refreshments and, out of pity (having also taken part in book signings in my time), I bought a copy of *Taviscombe Revisited*, signed by the author.

"Of course, your cottage is really old, isn't it?" Alison suddenly materialized at my elbow. "Our house is quite new—well, I think it was built about 1980 or thereabouts. I would have liked an old property, something thatched, you know, but Maurice is so practical—he said there would always be something that needed doing to it."

"As far as thatch is concerned," I said with feeling, "there always is."

"That cottage poor Eva bought, that was old, wasn't it? A bit remote for me but she seemed happy there. So sad. And her son, poor Daniel, is he staying for long?"

"I don't really know."

"Someone said he seemed quite settled there."

"Really?"

"I heard he was spending a lot of time with Rosemary's mother. I suppose he's interested in the family. This often happens, doesn't it, when someone dies? Poor Eva told me she was doing some research about it on the Internet. Perhaps he is carrying on with that? It's really very interesting—people get quite absorbed in it."

"I really don't know. Do excuse me," I said, edging away. "I really must go and see to things in the kitchen."

Gathering up some discarded cups and plates, I made my escape. I was peacefully washing up when Rosemary came in looking very ruffled.

"I'm absolutely fed up," she said.

"What's the matter?"

"Well, for one thing, Anthea's being quite impossible," she said. "She's going on about the refreshments—says they weren't *adequate*. I told her that if she'd let me know in time how many tickets she'd sold, we'd have known how many people we had to cater for."

"And what did she say?"

"Completely ignored me as usual, of course, and swept off to persecute poor Derek."

"Well, he can hold his own. So what else?"

"Oh, that tiresome Alison Shelby buttonholed me and kept going on about poor Eva and poor Daniel. It was all I could do not to be thoroughly rude to her."

"Yes, she is a menace. She got hold of me so I had to take refuge in here."

"You're all right in here," Rosemary said sourly. "She's always talking, but you never see her doing anything useful like washing up."

"Well, thank goodness for that," I said. "At least we're safe in here. Anyway," I said, "I'm more or less finished, so let's slip out the back way and go home for a restorative drink."

Daniel and Patrick seemed settled at the cottage, keeping themselves to themselves and not really taking part in Taviscombe life. Daniel continued to visit Mrs. Dudley (much to Rosemary's delight—"I've never known Mother so easy—it's wonderful!") and occasionally having supper with Rosemary and Jack.

"They're actually getting down to going through Alan's papers," Rosemary said. "Patrick's doing, of course. But I think Daniel is becoming really involved. He never seemed to be interested in his father's work."

"Odd, really," I said. "I mean, you'd think he'd be fascinated by all the adventures Alan had in those exotic places. Michael would have boasted about them to all the other boys."

"Yes, it was strange. Eva always thought that he'd sort of withdrawn himself from his father's job because he was afraid something would happen to him."

"Didn't want to get too close so that he wouldn't be hurt?"

"Something like that."

"But such a grown-up way of thinking about things when he was so young!"

"Daniel was always grown-up, in many ways. He never had friends of his own age, only really liked to be with adults. Patrick is the first person, the first contemporary, he's ever connected with."

"And *he's* odd too," I said. "Well, it's splendid that they've found each other."

"Eva was very relieved. She and Daniel were never close—she did try, but, again, he sort of held aloof. All part of the same thing, I suppose. So, after he was grown up and had his own life, she became more and more involved in her own work."

"Which she was very good at."

"Very good. And I suppose they drifted apart."

"I don't think I could have done that," I said thoughtfully.

"I certainly couldn't," Rosemary said. "But Eva was the sort of person who could detach herself from situations. You remember how she was, all those years ago, when Lassie, her beautiful collie, was run over? You and I would have been in floods, but she just *accepted* it, and we all knew how absolutely devoted she was to that dog."

"I suppose it's good to be like that. I mean, I'm sure she grieved as much as we would, but she was able to focus on other things. If you think about it, she was like that when Alan died."

"True. With Daniel she recognized how things were and simply got on with her life as he was getting on with his. It didn't mean she loved him any less."

"I suppose that's how she coped with Alan's job," I said. "All the being away and the danger."

"You're probably right. But," she went on firmly, "it wouldn't do for me."

I'd had a tiring afternoon's shopping in Taunton. Tiring and frustrating. I'd set out, not without hope, to buy a brown corduroy skirt. I should have known better. Plenty of brown skirts, also a few corduroy skirts, but never, of course, that particular combination. I should have learned from experience. A few years ago I wanted a red skirt. But, though I persevered for several months, there was never one of the right size, shape or shade of red (you'd be surprised how many shades of red there are). Eventually, when I had given up, I found it—perfect in every way. Exactly what I'd been looking for. But, by then, I felt I'd actually *had* a red skirt. So I didn't buy it. Exhausted by my fruitless search, I came to rest in rather a nice tea shop that had just opened and comforted myself with a pot of tea and a large piece of coffee and walnut cake.

I'd just settled down to enjoy it when I saw Maurice Shelby holding a tray and looking about him for an empty table. The tearoom was quite small and now very crowded. His eye lighted on me and he made his way toward me.

"May I join you?" he asked very formally.

"Of course," I said, though my heart rather sank at the thought of having to make conversation with him.

"It does get very busy in here," I said. "I suppose it's because it's only just opened and people want to see what it's like."

He nodded gravely, removed his plate and tea things from the tray, found nowhere to put it and replaced them.

"Oh dear," I said, "there's never anywhere to put the trays."

He nodded again and poured himself a cup of what looked like Earl Grey tea (no milk).

"Still," I said, "the cakes are delicious." I looked at his modest tea cake and felt, as I frequently do with Maurice Shelby, inadequate.

"I must say," he said with a smile, "your cake looks much more inviting than this."

Encouraged by the smile I said, "I've had a very frustrating afternoon so this is comfort eating."

"I suppose this"—he poked the tea cake with his fork—"is my version of the same thing, but rather inadequate for the purpose."

"Have you had a frustrating afternoon too?"

"Frustrating might be an extreme way of describing it—let us say tiresome."

Since there was no way I could inquire further, I concentrated on my cake.

"I was so very sorry to hear of the death of your friend," he said. "I would have spoken to you about it sooner but, as you know, such things are not easy to speak about at Brunswick Lodge."

"I know what you mean."

"I was a great admirer of her husband's work; he seemed to me a remarkable man, and she must have been remarkable too, to have lived with that kind of uncertainty."

"Yes, she was."

"I did not know she had a son. It must have been very hard for her to bring him up knowing that his father was in constant danger."

"Daniel was a very self-contained boy," I said. "Very old for his age. I think he knew and accepted the situation in a mature way."

"Remarkable. And now his mother has gone too, and so tragically. Does he have any other family?"

"Not close family. Rosemary is his nearest relation and she's some sort of cousin many times removed."

"Very sad."

"It's strange," I said. "Since Eva's gone, he's suddenly shown an interest in the family—previous generations, that is. Eva had started to look things up on the Internet and I think he's going to carry on where she left off."

"Really?"

I poured myself another cup of tea. "I believe you are interested in tracing your family too. Alison did mention it," I added, in case he thought I was just prying.

"Yes, indeed. I have always had an interest in genealogy over the years. I wish I had time to pursue it further."

"It's become so popular nowadays. I suppose because it's so much easier with the Internet and you no longer have to go around looking at church registers."

"Church registers can be most illuminating," he said, "and, when you actually handle them, you have the feeling of being in touch with the past in a way that simply looking up facts on a computer can never give you."

"Yes, you're right," I said, surprised at this very human attitude in someone I'd always regarded as lacking this quality. Though, to be fair, I'd hardly ever had any conversation with him and regarded him simply as an adjunct to his tiresome wife. "Like when you actually put your hand on a really ancient stone pillar," I said, "and can feel the hands that have touched it before you. Years ago, before they fenced it off so you can't get anywhere near it, I used to stop at Stonehenge whenever we were driving up to London—before the motorway when you had to go the long way round. I used to touch the stones to feel the connection. I suppose I shouldn't have done that," I added hastily. "If everyone had done it . . ."

"It's turned into a theme park now," he said. "The mystery and the magic have gone. I'm glad you had a chance to see it properly."

He finished the last of his tea cake. "I must return to the office; I don't normally go out in the middle of the afternoon, but it has been a difficult day." He got up. "Thank you for your company and your conversation." He inclined his head in a sort of salute and departed.

For a while I sat there, my tea going cold, thinking, tritely, that first impressions can be wrong.

"He was quite human," I said to Rosemary, "actually conversable. I was really surprised."

"He was probably glad of a little rational conversation after living with that wife of his."

"I suppose that now his daughters have left home it must be a bit tedious for him. I can't think why he married her!"

"Mother said that she had money and that always helps."

"Yes, of course, he's on his own, isn't he, now his partner has gone? I'm surprised he never merged with a larger firm. Michael said it's quite a good practice. A lot of work with wills and trusts. People who like an old-fashioned setup, not all this timed interviews and such."

"Well, good luck to him—everything's too high-powered for me nowadays. Which reminds me: Mother's decided there's something wrong with her glasses—I don't think there is; she's only had them for a short while—so I have to take her to see Mr. Melhuish. Fortunately he's used to her after all these years so he takes it all in his stride."

"Of course," I said, "that was where she first met Donald Webster, wasn't it? Does she still see him?"

"Not so often since Eva died. I don't think he goes anywhere much now. It's very sad. He seems to have retreated inside himself."

"I suppose it's not surprising; after all he wanted to marry her."

"True. Still, Mother doesn't miss him that much now she's so occupied with Dan and Patrick."

"Patrick as well?"

"Mostly Dan, but Patrick sometimes goes along too. I think Mother's rather intrigued about him—she's never met anyone so self-contained before."

"What does he think about Daniel's preoccupation with all the family stuff?"

"He encourages it; even helps a bit with the genealogy search—Dan's not much good with the Internet."

"I can imagine. Have they got very far yet?"

"Dan's not bothering with all that while he's been going over all those photos and stuff with Mother. It's really been so good for her. Of course she was upset over Eva, and she'd got a bit down. Having Dan around seems to have given her a new lease of life, thank goodness."

"I think it's done a lot for him as well."

"Thank goodness for that too."

"Going back to Donald," I said, after a moment. "I'm a bit concerned about him. I suppose it's not surprising that he's withdrawn. After all, he's got no one to talk to about Eva. I think, just for a start, I might invite him to supper. That is, if you and Jack will come too."

"You don't think that might be a bit embarrassing

for him? I mean, I wasn't very friendly to him while he was seeing Eva."

"No, I think he'd like it if you were there. And if Jack comes too there can be general conversation, not just talking about her. It's just a way of breaking the ice, as it were."

"Well, if you think it'll be all right, let me know when you want us."

"The sooner the better, really. I don't like to think of him shut away and grieving."

Chapter Eleven

Actually, it all went off very well. I think Donald was glad to be with other people again and he was obviously trying to be his old sociable self. We did talk about Eva, but in a general way and not for too long. Fortunately Jack and Donald got on very well—in fact by the end of the evening they'd arranged a date to play golf together.

"Many thanks to you both," I said to Rosemary. "It went off very well and I do think it helped Donald."

"Jack certainly took to him—he's very choosy who he plays golf with!"

"Oh, that was really splendid; I was so grateful."

"Well, he's quite an interesting person when you get to know him," Rosemary said. "I can see now how he and Eva would have got along. I just wish it could have happened."

I was glad to think that I'd managed to help Donald, even if it was only marginally. Time may be a great healer, but, as I knew myself, it was a slow process.

After that evening I was suddenly very busy. Michael had to go up to London for some legal business and suggested that Thea should go with him for a little break. So Alice came to stay with me. Which was lovely, but I'd forgotten how much there is to do for the young. Back and forth to school, back and forth to the many out-of-school activities, back and forth to birthday parties, homework to supervise, and meals to be ready at specific times, not just when I felt like getting them.

"*And*," I said to Maureen when I explained that I couldn't possibly go to a committee meeting at Brunswick Lodge, "I have a review I promised for next week and I haven't even had time to read the book yet. So apologies for my absence, please."

I was trying to persuade Alice to have a second piece of toast (she's just at the age when girls don't think breakfast is cool) when the phone rang. It was Rosemary. At first I could hardly make out what she was saying, she was so incoherent. Eventually she calmed down a little.

"It's so *terrible*, I can't think straight. Oh, Sheila, it's dreadful."

"Rosemary, what's the matter?"

"It's Daniel—he's dead!"

"What? What do you mean, dead?"

"Knocked down by a car." She was overcome and sobbing now.

"Is Jack there?"

"He's gone to help Patrick—he wouldn't let me go . . ."

"Look, hold on. I'll be right over—at least, I have to take Alice to school but I'll come straight on from there. Oh, Rosemary, I'm *so* sorry. Hold on!"

I hustled Alice into the car, ignoring her protests that she'd be frightfully early, dropped her off at school and drove to Rosemary. She was still tearful but more herself.

"I still can't take it in." She was trembling and I put my arms around her and we sat quietly for a while.

"A cup of tea?" I asked. "Or something stronger?"

"Tea, please."

When I got back with the tray she was calmer.

"When did it happen?"

She shook her head as if to clear it.

"This morning, very early. He went out running—he'd been doing that every day. When he didn't come back Patrick went to look for him and when he found him . . ."

"How horrible."

"Patrick called an ambulance, but they said he was—he was dead."

"The driver didn't stop?"

"No, they had to call the police. Oh, Sheila, it's so awful—how could anyone!"

"That's unspeakable!"

Rosemary sat in silent misery and there seemed nothing I could say so I poured the tea and persuaded her to drink a little of it.

Quite soon Jack came back. "Rosie, are you all right—thank you for coming, Sheila—I hated to leave you." Rosemary nodded and Jack went on. "The police came and they're looking for tire marks and doing what they have to do." He put his arm around her. "They'll get the bastard—there's a lot they can do now. They'll get him all right."

"What time did Daniel go out?" I asked. "I mean, was it properly light?"

"It was light and not foggy—there's no excuse," Jack said fiercely. "Someone coming back from a night out—drunk, probably."

"How's Patrick?" I asked.

"Shaken, of course, but calm and practical—like he always is. I couldn't have coped like he did." He turned to Rosemary. "Do you want me to tell your mother?"

She sighed. "No, I'll do it—but not just yet."

"Is there anything I can do?" I asked helplessly. "Get you both some breakfast, anything?"

"No, really," Rosemary said. "We're all right. I'll phone you later on when we know a bit more."

I left them sitting together in silence.

When I got home I couldn't settle to anything. I did some housework, cooked food for the animals, prepared supper for Alice and me. I was glad Michael and Thea would be back the next day—I wanted to be free to do anything I could for Rosemary. Finally, at lunchtime, I sat down with a sandwich and took in the full reality of what had happened. First Alan, then Eva, and now Daniel—a succession of terrible things happening within such a short space of time. Alan's death was, of course, natural, but both Eva and Daniel had died because of cruel accidents—well, Daniel's death wasn't an accident, but there seemed no chance of ever finding the person responsible. It was so unfair. Life was unfair. But still . . . I sat for a long time, in the kind of numb state where you don't really think of anything, don't even feel anything. You just sit, simply existing. I was roused by the sound of the phone. I leaped to my feet expecting Rosemary, but it was a cold-caller asking me if I'd recently had an accident and would like to claim compensation. I threw away the uneaten sandwich and went to collect Alice from school. I didn't hear anything from Rosemary and I was glad to have Alice to look after. I told her about Daniel, as simply as I could and, fortunately, she took it very well. Before supper we took Tris for a walk high up on West Hill, and as I looked down at the late, thin sunlight glistening on the sea below I found a sort of peace.

I didn't see much of Rosemary for the next few days. She spent a lot of time with Patrick, arranging the funeral, and it seemed to help her.

"It's good to have something I can *do*," she said when she phoned me briefly. "Patrick's been amazing. Not just over the funeral, but with Mother."

"How is she?" I asked. "It must have been a dreadful blow—she'd become so fond of him."

"She was dreadfully upset. Really quite ill. If it hadn't been for Patrick . . . He's spent every minute he could spare from making all the arrangements with her. I was so grateful, especially when he must be feeling so devastated himself."

"How is he?"

"Calm, as you'd expect, not showing any sort of emotion, but just getting on with things, as efficient as ever."

"What will he do? After, I mean. Has he said anything?"

"No, and, of course, I haven't asked."

"Have you heard anything from the police?"

"Nothing, really. They just said that they were continuing to make inquiries. Apparently, because there hadn't been any rain for quite a while, there weren't usable tire marks, and at that time in the morning there weren't people about, especially along that lane, which is very quiet anyway."

"They'll find something," I said without much hope.

"Even if they do," Rosemary said sadly, "it won't bring him back."

There weren't many people at the funeral, just the family and some of Rosemary's friends. Donald was there and I was pleased to see a few from Brunswick Lodge. As we stood by the newly dug grave, it seemed almost unbearably poignant to think how very recently we had stood at Eva's nearby. It was painful to see Mrs. Dudley supported by Patrick, as she had been supported by Daniel not so long ago. There was no formal gathering afterward and people slipped quietly away, leaving the family to say their last good-byes alone. After the funeral, Jack took Rosemary away for a few days and when they returned we all tried to get on with things as best we could.

I was in the library looking aimlessly at the display of DVDs that seemed, with the computers, to be taking over from the books, when a familiar voice behind me said, "Is there anything any good?"

It was Inspector Morris, Bob Morris, whom I'd known as a little boy and who used to come with his father to work in my garden.

"Bob! I haven't seen you for ages. How are you, and how is your father?"

"I'm fine and so's Dad. He's been a different person since he had that hip operation. That was thanks to you persuading him."

"I'm so glad he decided to do it."

There was a pause and then he said, "I was so sorry about that young friend of yours. Hit-and-run driving is particularly bad—especially for the relatives."

"Is there any hope of finding who did it?" I asked.

He shook his head. "Not so far. The road conditions weren't any help in identifying the car, and on a country lane at that time of day—well, there's very little chance of any witness. We've put out appeals, of course, but nothing so far, and, to be honest, there's very little chance of anything now. I'm so sorry."

"Was there any chance of identifying the car from Daniel's injuries?"

"Not really. It was almost instantaneous. It must have been a large vehicle, possibly a four-by-four, and there were no fragments of paint on the body so he was probably struck by some metal part on the front of the vehicle, one of those bull bars they have on large Land Rovers, perhaps. It may not have left any very noticeable marks on the vehicle." He paused. "I'm so sorry," he repeated.

"It's been particularly painful," I said, "because his mother, Eva, Eva Jackson, died so recently—that was dreadful because she shouldn't have died."

"Eva Jackson, that name rings a bell."

"She died in a diabetic coma, but no one knew for days. There was an inquest."

"Yes, of course, I remember it now. That was a tragic thing to happen. So she was this boy's mother?"

"She was an old friend of mine and had just come back to Taviscombe after her husband died. So you see, it's been one terrible thing after another."

"I'm really sorry. I wish I could be more positive about the hit and run. We'll keep it open, of course, and I'll let you know if anything turns up."

"Thank you." I turned toward the display of DVDs. "Are you looking for anything special?"

"Dad wanted to see that series about a Victorian

kitchen garden. He missed it when it was on TV. But I don't think they've got it here."

"Oh, I've got a copy of that," I said. "I'll take it round—it would be nice to see him again."

I was pleased to see Bob's father looking quite spry.

"Made all the difference, that operation," he said. "Glad you made me see sense about it. I can do all sorts now, out in the garden too—one less thing I've got to ask Bob to do."

"That's splendid."

"He's so busy nowadays; I don't like bothering him all the time. That's the trouble about getting old, having to rely on other people—it's not fair on the children."

"I'm sure they want to help," I said.

"They're willing enough, but it's having to ask. That's why that operation was a marvel—it gave me back a bit of my independence."

"I know. You don't like to keep asking the children to do things, although they always say they want to help. But young people lead such busy lives now and have so much on their mind. You must feel that with Bob, especially with his job."

"That I do. He and Molly will do anything for me, and always so cheerful about it. But Bob's always been a worrier and this job really takes it out of him sometimes. Only the other day—well, he never talks about his cases to me, but I could tell he had something on his mind and when I asked him, he said it was nothing, just he felt there was something not right with one of his cases, couldn't put his finger on it. He shut up then, like he always does. But I could see it was bothering him."

"That must happen quite often," I said. "Especially with someone as conscientious as Bob."

"He's always been a thoughtful lad, one of the quiet ones."

"Yes, I remember."

He picked up the DVD. "And it was very thoughtful of you, Mrs. Malory, to bring this. It's something I always wanted to see, how they did things in the old days, and I missed it when it first came round. I'll watch it straightaway and get it back to you."

"No, you keep it. I've got so many things I mean to watch and never seem to have the time. Anyway, it's worth looking at more than once!"

Rosemary and I were driving over the moor to have lunch in Exford, something we do sometimes when we feel in the need of a little break. It was bright and sunny, not too hot, as we drove over Porlock Common, and, when we stopped to look at some foals in the group of Exmoor ponies grazing near the road, there was a refreshing breeze.

"It really is a perfect day," Rosemary said, looking at the view in front of us, steep wooded valleys and stretches of moorland dotted with sheep. "You can see for miles."

"Yes," I agreed. "I couldn't bear to live anywhere else. I mean, other places are fine to visit, but this—well, this is where I belong."

"I think Eva felt that—that was why she came back—and I think Daniel was beginning to feel a sort of pull . . ."

I was silent for a moment, then I asked, "What about Patrick? Is he going back to London?"

She shook her head. "I don't think so, not yet, anyway—he hasn't said anything. He doesn't seem to be thinking beyond the next day. I know he's so composed and *together* but he seems somehow lost without Daniel. Not surprising, they were very close. Of course the cottage belongs to him now."

"Really?"

"Well, Eva left everything to Daniel and apparently Daniel made a will ages ago leaving everything to Patrick."

"I see."

"There'll be two lots of death duties, but I don't think he'd need to sell the cottage to cover them, so he could stay on here if he wanted to."

"How would you feel about that?"

"We've had a lot to do with him lately and I've grown very fond of him, and he's been amazing with Mother. I suppose it's because he's a link with Daniel."

"But what about his life in London?"

"I suppose Daniel *was* his life there. He doesn't seem to have any family and I think his friends were people he knew through Daniel. He's already canceled all Daniel's commitments—his column and television stuff, all the business side of things. He did that straightaway—efficient as always. Sometimes I wish he'd show some sort of emotion—I'm sure he's grieving, and perhaps he gives way when he's alone. I don't know. I just wish I could help him."

"It may be a help for him to stay on here. In a way, you're the only family he's got."

Chapter Twelve

I was having a quick snack in the Buttery when Donald appeared beside me.

"Thank goodness," he said. "A sympathetic ear." He put his tray down and sank heavily into his chair.

"What on earth . . ."

"Anthea. Need I say more!"

"What particular horror has she perpetrated this time?"

"She's trapped me into giving another Little Talk. I did struggle—believe me, I really did—but she just tanked over me. Wore me down—I'm absolutely shattered."

"Well," I said, "it had to happen sometime. You'll feel better when it's over."

"That is not the sympathy I was looking for."

I laughed. "We've all been there, and you're a bigger catch than most. Apart from that, how are you?"

"Oh, I don't know. A bit lost, I suppose; I'd just arranged my life and then it fell into pieces. I don't really know what I want to do."

"But you don't want to leave Taviscombe?"

"In some ways—make a clean break. But I've settled here, made a few friends, as well as . . ."

"I know. It must be hard."

"Thank you. Since Eva . . . went, I haven't been able to think clearly. There's nowhere else I need to be. No family, well, no close family. I suppose I might as well be here as anywhere."

"We'd miss you if you did go. You do seem to have become part of the community."

"Giving a little talk at Brunswick Lodge?"

"You brought a bit of fresh air from the outside world to our little circle. Not just that—you're on the committee and, if you wanted to, there are masses of things you could be involved in."

"I don't know that I'm a committee sort of person— I only got involved because of Eva."

"What would you do if you went somewhere else? Travel?"

"I don't know what I'd do. I was sick of travel— that's why I came here when I more or less retired, to get some sort of stability."

"Well, then. No, seriously, you'd be missed, and not just for committees and things. Anyway, you've promised to play golf with Jack—that's a sort of stability."

"He and Rosemary are nice people—I'd like to get to know them better."

"And there's Mrs. Dudley."

"Yes. Poor soul, she must be dreadfully upset. First Eva and now Daniel."

"Daniel's death hit her very hard—they'd become very close. He was beginning to show an interest in the family and she loved getting out the old photos and telling him stories about past family members, usually to their disadvantage. They had a high old time."

"How is she?"

"She was quite ill for a while, but then Patrick took to going to see her and that seemed to help a lot."

"Oh yes, Patrick. Eva used to say how good he was for Daniel, but I never really got a picture of him, if you know what I mean."

"I don't think anyone does," I said. "He's always polite and charming in an understated sort of way, but you don't ever know what he's thinking or how he's really reacting to things. We're used to him as Daniel's shadow, without any sort of personality of his own, which is ridiculous because I do feel that there's a great deal there, under the surface."

"What will he do now?"

"I don't think anyone knows. Daniel left him the cottage, so he seems to be staying on there."

"Left him the cottage?"

"He left everything to Patrick. There weren't any close relations—well, there's Rosemary and her family and Mrs. Dudley, but they're not exactly close. And he and Patrick—well. Anyway, I gather he'd made the will ages ago." I sighed. "He was so young, such a waste of a promising life."

"I suppose," Donald said, "we should be grateful that Eva wasn't alive when it happened; it would have destroyed her. But then, if she'd still been alive he wouldn't have been at the cottage and that dreadful accident would never have happened—oh, I don't know. It's all so complicated!"

"You must never say 'what if,'" I said. "It only leads to useless regrets."

"You're right, but sometimes you can't help dwelling on it."

I was thinking of what Donald had been saying about the sequence of events and the cottage as I walked down toward the harbor. I stopped abruptly when I saw a young man leaning on the sea wall precisely where I'd seen Daniel all those weeks ago. As I drew nearer I saw that it was Patrick. For a moment I hesitated, then I went toward him.

He greeted me with his usual half smile and said, "This was one of Dan's favorite places."

"I know," I replied. "I saw him here not long ago and he told me about the shipping forecast. We discovered we shared an addiction to it."

Patrick smiled—a genuine smile this time. "I was very rarely awake that early."

"I'm so sorry," I said. "There's nothing to say, I know, except the trite things about needing to grieve and time being a great healer. But it is, though you may not think so now."

He nodded slightly, in acknowledgment, and was silent for a moment, so that I wondered if I ought to go away and leave him to his thoughts.

Suddenly he said, "I can't grieve when I feel like this."

"You must feel very angry," I said.

"Not just angry—though, goodness knows I feel that—but there's this feeling . . ."

"Feeling?"

"That it wasn't an accident."

"You mean that someone ran him down deliberately? But who on earth . . ."

"I know, it's completely irrational, but there it is."

"But even if there *was* somebody," I said, "how could they know where he'd be and that he'd be there, out on that particular road at that particular time?"

He shook his head. "I know all that, but still, there are things that make me wonder. It's such a co-incidence that *anyone* should have been driving down that road so early in the morning. And Dan must have been perfectly visible. It was a straight stretch of road, so it wasn't someone coming round a corner and coming on him suddenly. There was a bit of early morning mist, but not enough to count, and his track-suit was navy so it would have showed up against the road."

The words came pouring out, as if he'd been re-luctant to utter them.

"I believe the police think it might have been some-one coming back drunk after a night out," I said.

"Yes, I know. But they must have known what they'd done," he went on. "They *must* have done, and then to drive on—how could they do that? He might have still been alive. I can't stop thinking about it—if only I'd known . . ."

He was silent for a moment and looked at me thoughtfully, as if trying to decide whether to con-tinue. Then he said, "I have a feeling the police think there's something wrong too. At least, it seemed to me that inspector has some sort of doubt about it."

"Bob Morris? I wonder . . ."

Patrick looked at me sharply. "What is it?"

"It may not be—"

"What is it?" he repeated. "Please tell me."

"I know Bob's father quite well," I said, "and when we were talking the other day, he happened to mention that Bob had something on his mind, some-thing not quite right about one of his cases."

"You see!"

"It may very well have been one of his other cases."

"I must speak to him."

"I don't know—I had no right to repeat some-thing his father said."

"I won't mention that," he said impatiently, "but if he already has a doubt, surely there must be something more he can do."

"He's an intelligent, sympathetic man so I'm sure he'll listen to what you have to say, but don't get your hopes too high. I'm sure he'll have covered every possibility—he's very thorough."

"But if he's been approaching it from the wrong angle," Patrick said eagerly, "thinking of it as a simple accident."

"But if there's no motive?"

"We don't *know* that—there may be something we have no idea about."

"But you know him so well, surely you would have heard if there'd been anything like that."

"How can we say we know everything about anyone?" he said and I thought how ironic that was, coming from him.

"Well, have a word with him," I said.

"Yes, I will." He paused and, for a moment, it looked as if he was going to resume his usual formal manner, but then he said, "Thank you for listening to me." His voice was uncertain. "I can talk to you—not many people—sometimes not even Dan . . . Thank you, Mrs. Malory."

"Sheila, please. Let me know what Bob Morris says and do remember that I'm always there if you do want to talk. And you know that anything you tell me will remain just between us. Now I'll leave you to look at the sea."

* * *

I thought about Patrick a lot when I got home. It was so unlike him to speak in such an unguarded way. He must have felt very strongly to have unburdened himself like that. I was obscurely flattered, as one is when a timid animal lets you approach it. And, of course, I kept thinking about what he'd said about Daniel's death not being an accident.

It was just possible that was what Bob Morris had been worrying about. Looking at the facts dispassionately, it *did* seem strange that someone, however drunk, hadn't been aware of Daniel in the road, though I suppose he (one somehow assumed it was a he) might have just panicked. And there seemed to be no possible reason for anyone to want Daniel dead. There would have to be an overpowering reason for someone to deliberately drive a car straight at another human being and leave him for dead. I shuddered when I thought of it. But *who* could have wanted Daniel dead? If Patrick couldn't think of anyone . . .

My mind kept going round in unprofitable circles and I was quite glad when Foss, jumping up onto the worktop, knocked down a jug of milk and I had to spend a considerable time clearing it up, knowing, from bitter experience, that unless you track spilled milk down to the remotest corner it will remain there and generate the most unpleasant smell.

Rosemary called round later in the day and I

wished I could tell her about my conversation with Patrick, but, of course, I couldn't. Instead I asked if she knew how long he might be staying at the cottage.

"No idea. Nobody's actually asked him, but I do hope he stays a good long time—Mother's come to rely on him."

"What do they talk about?" I asked curiously.

"The Old Days. That is, Mother tells him about how life was—better, of course—when she was young and how well everyone behaved during the War."

"Goodness! And Patrick likes this?"

"Do you know, I believe he does. I mean, he asks intelligent questions, as if he really wants to know."

"Well, good for Patrick."

"I think," Rosemary said, "though I may be wildly wrong, that he quite likes feeling that he's part of a family."

"We have no idea, I suppose, about his own family?"

"No idea at all. We know he originally came from Ireland—though not how long ago—but that's all. I suppose Eva might have known a bit more about him, though she was always very relaxed about Daniel's friends.

"And," I said, "he's very much *not* the sort of person you ask personal questions."

"That's true."

"What's he going to do about the London flat?"

"I think he'll sell it."

"But surely he'll need somewhere to live when he

goes back there. I mean, he'll need another job and London's the place where his sort of job would be."

"He doesn't seem to have thought about that. He seems to be in a sort of limbo, living one day at a time."

"Of course, he and Daniel were very close—it wasn't just a business relationship. I suppose he can't really imagine life without him."

"He's really disoriented. I suppose he's just clinging to anything connected with Daniel."

"Like your mother."

"Well, yes."

"How is she?"

"I'm really worried about her—she's very much not herself. She enjoys Patrick coming but, just lately, she seems to have lost interest in things. She didn't even seem interested in the Muriel Masters story."

"Muriel? What's that?"

"Oh, she and Dennis are separating."

"Good heavens, after thirty years!"

"Well that's what Muriel says, but you know what she's like. They were going to be divorced eight years ago, but nothing ever came of it."

"But *why*? Dennis isn't seeing anyone else?"

"No, nothing like that. She just says she wants to go and live in Spain."

"And Dennis doesn't want to?"

"Dennis in Spain! No, it's just another of her 'I'm so bored' things and she wants to liven things up a bit—you know what she's like."

"And your mother wasn't interested in *that*?"

"No—well, there was a flicker but she just couldn't be bothered."

"There must be something wrong."

"Yes. Seriously, though, I think I'll get Dr. Horobin to have a look at her."

Chapter Thirteen

Dr. Horobin's verdict was that Mrs. Dudley had had a slight stroke. "Not unusual at her age," he said briskly, "but she must take care."

Needless to say, Mrs. Dudley was very scathing. "It's perfectly ridiculous. I think I would have known if something as important as that had happened—or does Dr. Horobin"—immense scorn at the mention of his name)—"believe he knows more about me than I know myself? He's only been my doctor for a very short time. Dr. Macdonald was my doctor for many years and *he* would never have dreamed of saying such a thing."

"She's being absolutely impossible," Rosemary said wearily. "I suppose she's in denial, or whatever the phrase is. And she refuses to do any of the things that might help—it really is so difficult. She had a mild stroke years ago and Dr. Horobin says that this one may well be the first of several or even a possible major one. I'm at my wits' end!"

A second stroke, however, which left her with some loss of movement, persuaded her that she was, indeed, in need of specialist care and she agreed to go into hospital ("I shall go privately, of course") for treatment.

"Such a relief. She's being difficult, of course, but, since she's paying to be looked after she's much more inclined to do what they say," Rosemary said. "Of course, it means I have to go up to Taunton every day, but it's such a relief to know she's under cover."

"Do you think she'd like a visit?" I asked.

"Oh, would you? It's not just seeing people—though, of course, she enjoys that—but it's a matter of prestige how many visitors you have."

Mrs. Dudley was watching the racing on television when I arrived. At least the television was on but she had dozed off and I was shocked to see how frail she looked, leaning back in her chair. But as the nurse ushered me into her room she woke up, almost her old self, looking critically at the pot plant (a white cyclamen) and the lavender water I had brought. These, apparently, were approved and she greeted me in her usual brisk manner.

"Well, Sheila, it was good of you to spare time from your busy life to pay me a visit. Now you've arrived we can have tea." The last words were addressed to the nurse, who retreated hastily, and she went on, "The food here is tolerable but not, of course, what I am used to at home. Now then, tell me what has been happening. Rosemary is useless, always dashing off somewhere, she never has time for a really good chat."

I was pleased that she seemed to have regained her appetite for gossip and I'd come prepared with various items that I hoped would catch her attention. The appearance of a young girl with the tea things provoked sharp comments.

"No, not there. My visitor will pour—put it down *there*, on that table. Goodness gracious," she went on when the girl was barely out of the room, "the service here is *not* what you might expect given the exorbitant charges they make for everything." She took up a sandwich and regarded it disapprovingly. "Egg and cress again. And the cakes aren't much better. The macaroons are tolerable but I can't recommend the Victoria sponge."

I poured the tea and took one of the despised sandwiches and said, "Oh well, Elsie's Victoria sponges are very special."

She sighed heavily. "You see what I have to put up with."

However, I was pleased to see that she ate quite a few of the sandwiches and a large piece of Dundee cake. We had just finished when a nurse appeared.

"Now, Mrs. Dudley, it's time for your physio."

"I can't possibly go now. I have a visitor."

"You know it's only a fifteen-minute session; I'm sure your visitor won't mind waiting."

I awaited with interest the outcome of this little interchange, saying, "Of course you must go—I'm happy to wait."

There was a pregnant silence for a full minute, then Mrs. Dudley rose reluctantly, heaving herself out of her chair with exaggerated movements.

"Fifteen minutes, Sheila," she said sharply, and slowly followed the nurse out of the room.

Since I never travel anywhere without a book, I fished a copy of *Barchester Towers* from my bag and settled down to read. After a few minutes the young girl came in to clear away the tea things. She glanced curiously at the book in my hand.

"Is that a good book?" she inquired.

"Yes," I replied, "a very good book." Feeling unable to elaborate on this judgment, I asked, "Do you read much?"

"I read Harry Potter. That was a good book."

"I believe it was."

"I went to that *Lord of the Rings* film and my boyfriend got the book of it, but neither of us could make head or tail of it."

"What was the problem?"

She gathered up the last of the cups onto the tray. "Too many words," she said and went away. Slightly unnerved by this exchange, I returned to Trollope.

When Mrs. Dudley came back I thought she looked tired and made as if to go, but she said irritably that I'd only just got there and there were things she wanted to talk to me about.

I sat down obediently and waited. She made a

great fuss about settling back into her chair, saying that she was exhausted by having been Pulled About, but eventually she said, "It's about Patrick. I want you to talk to him."

"Me? What about?"

"I want you to make sure he's going to be staying on at the cottage."

"Wouldn't it be more suitable if Rosemary asked him?"

"That would look as if she wanted him to go."

"Well, I did speak to him a little while ago and he seemed to be settled there then."

She was silent for a while, then she said, "Now that Daniel's gone . . ." She paused. "Patrick has very good manners, a most unusual young man, always so interested in what I have to tell him. There's no need for him to go back to London—he has the cottage and the money Daniel left him." She looked at me almost anxiously. "He seems to be happy down here—I'm sure I've heard him say so many times."

"Yes," I said gently, "he seems to be. I don't believe he's thinking of moving—for a while, at least."

As I drove home I thought of the way Patrick had gradually become so important to Mrs. Dudley. Not as important as Daniel, but a sort of substitute for him. And, of course, she couldn't ask Rosemary to sound him out about staying in Taviscombe. There's no way she'd want Rosemary to know how much he meant to her. But was Patrick, I wondered, really that interested in her endless stories of the old days? It seemed unlikely. If not, what did he have to gain from his attentions and his constant visits? It wasn't as if he had monetary expectations—as she had pointed out, Daniel had left him well provided for and somehow I didn't feel that he cared too much about money anyway. Perhaps he just liked her, but it was an improbable relationship, especially given Mrs. Dudley's acerbic manner.

What Patrick had said about Daniel's death not being an accident came back to me when I saw Bob Morris coming out of the police station a few days later. I was on the other side of the road and didn't have an opportunity to speak to him about it, but it set me thinking and I wondered if Patrick had actually spoken to him about it and, if so, what his reaction had been. Why on earth would anyone want to kill Daniel? Local people hardly knew him and it was unlikely, to say the least of it, that someone would have followed him down from London for the purpose. No, Patrick must have been wrong, but then, if it *was* Daniel's death that Bob Morris had been uncertain about . . .

I resolutely put it out of my mind and hurried along to Brunswick Lodge with the cakes I'd made for the Red Cross coffee morning. It was in full swing when I got there and Anthea accosted me as I came through the door.

"Oh, there you are," she said disapprovingly. "I couldn't think where you'd got to. Brenda Morrison's been waiting for ages to set up her stall." She unwrapped my offerings. "Oh dear, we already have two ginger cakes; I thought you were going to make a fruitcake. Well, I suppose we must manage somehow."

I got myself a cup of coffee and looked for somewhere to sit down. My heart sank when I saw Alison Shelby waving at me and reluctantly went and sat down beside her.

"What a squash," she said brightly. "Still it's lovely that so many people have turned out—such a good cause. I did a Red Cross first-aid course last year—well, I do think everyone should be able to help in an emergency. And, would you believe it, just a few weeks after I'd finished the course, Mrs. Shoulders, my daily, cut her hand so I was able to bind her up quite professionally. Of course, if it had been a really deep cut I'd have taken her to hospital; you can't be too careful. Oh, I meant to tell you—Anthea asked me to tell any of the committee members I happened to see that the meeting on Monday has been canceled. Derek can't make it and there's no point in having a meeting without the treasurer."

"No, of course not. I'll be quite glad not to—"

"It's Edna, his wife. She's making him go with her to the venue."

"The venue?"

"The wedding venue—for their daughter's wedding."

"Oh yes, I remember now . . ."

"I think it's that place just outside Porlock. Very nice, I'm sure, and not too pricey—well, Derek's always been careful with money, though you'd think for his only daughter! Of course when our girls were married, with Lydia marrying a barrister and Charlotte marrying an important doctor, we had to push the boat out, as they say. A lot of people down from London, so the actual ceremonies had to be at St. Mary's in Taunton—not enough room in our local church, though that would have been nice—then the reception was at the Castle Hotel, and that cost a pretty penny, I can tell you."

"I'm sure . . ."

"Of course, just having a son you didn't have all that bother—buy a new hat and you're done!"

I drank my coffee and let the flow of talk wash over me and fortunately Anthea came back to make sure I knew about the committee meeting so I was able to get away.

"I can't imagine how Maurice Shelby, who seems to be a sensible man, puts up with her," I said to Rosemary when I ran into her in the post office. "I'm absolutely exhausted after fifteen minutes of all that chat. How on earth does he bear it day after day?"

"I don't think he's home much these days," Rosemary said. "Since his partner's gone, he seems to be working all hours, so Jack says."

"And glad to! He doesn't seem like someone who would have been trapped by a pretty face—you can see that she must have been pretty when she was young—but, of course, there was the money. It probably seemed a reasonable price to pay."

"Well, he never seems to have much to say for

himself so perhaps she's got into the habit of chattering away to fill the silence!"

"Actually, if you remember, I did have a reasonable conversation with him in that tearoom in the precinct. I suspect that dry, precise manner hides a perfectly good sense of humor."

"'Precise' is the word," Rosemary said. "Matthew Philips was telling Jack only the other day how he fusses about things. Matthew, who's a bit of a stick-in-the-mud himself, has always had Maurice Shelby as his solicitor and he had to consult him about a legacy. A bit of a complication—the obvious beneficiary had gone abroad and though they advertised for him he hadn't turned up. Apparently there's a thing called beneficiary insurance, which means that if the person does eventually turn up after you've had the money, you can pay him back with the insurance. The legacy was only a small sum and Matthew didn't want the bother of it but Maurice Shelby was really insistent that they should do it, made quite a thing of it!"

"Yes, Michael says he's got the reputation of being a stickler for things like that, all the niggling detail. I don't think he has that many clients—old-fashioned—so I imagine it's mostly elderly people who've been with him for some time. It must be very difficult these days for someone in a single-person practice."

When I got home I still felt stifled by Alison's endless conversation and felt the need for some fresh air, so I got the lead and took Tris for a walk along the beach.

We both walk quite slowly now but there's something about the sea air that invigorates us. Tris wandered off to investigate clumps of seaweed and I walked right down to the water's edge to watch each little wave lapping on the hard ribbed sand. After a while it began to rain, lightly at first but suddenly very heavily. I gathered up Tris and made for one of the shelters. I was trying, ineffectually, to dry my hair, which was dripping onto my collar, when someone else came in. It was Patrick.

"What a day!" I exclaimed. "Are you very wet?"

"Not too bad. I made a dash for it."

Tris chose this moment to shake himself vigorously and we both became much wetter.

"I was so sorry about Mrs. Dudley's stroke," I said tentatively. "But she does seem to be making a good recovery."

"She was in good form when I saw her last week. Quite her old self."

"Yes, I thought that. I pity the nurses, though I suppose they're used to difficult patients." I paused for a moment and then went on, "It was very good of you to visit. It means a lot to her, you know."

"Yes, well, I know how much she must be missing Daniel; it seemed the least I could do."

"She's not an easy person but you both seem to get on really well."

"Oh, she just wants someone who'll listen. Someone new to tell her stories to."

"You're doing her a lot of good, especially just now. She'll miss you when you go."

He shook his head. "Oh, I'm not going, not until all this business about Daniel's death is sorted out."

"Did you speak to Inspector Morris? What did he say?"

"He was very noncommittal, but I still get the feeling that he's uneasy about it."

"Are they doing anything? Surely they're trying to find the driver?"

"I asked him, of course, and he said the case was still open but with no witnesses it's more or less impossible."

"I suppose so."

"It's ridiculous," he burst out. "They're still treating it as an accident."

"You told him you think it was deliberate?"

"Yes, but I couldn't give him any reason why anyone would want Daniel dead. No reason, no person—it's all so frustrating. But I just *know* it was deliberate and I'm sure he thinks so too. I don't know what to do, Sheila. That's why I want you to speak to him. You know him and he'll listen to you."

"I'll try, but, really, I have nothing more to say to him than you have."

"Please, Sheila!"

"I'll mention it to him when I see him, if that's any use. But I don't believe there's anything else he can do, whatever he may feel about it."

Chapter Fourteen

As it happened, I did run into Bob Morris in the library.

"Are you looking for gardening books for your father?" I asked casually.

"No, something on the First World War—there's been a lot on TV lately and he got interested."

"How is he? I really meant to drop in on him again but I seem to get caught up in things. And, of course, there's been all this terrible business about Daniel." I paused for a moment. "I believe Patrick, his partner, doesn't think it was an accident." I looked at him inquiringly.

"Well, not an accident, exactly—a hit-and-run."

"And you're no nearer finding the driver?"

"No witnesses—there hardly would be on that road at that time of day."

"Surely that's the point. Who *would* have been driving along there then?"

"Some drunk returning from a night out."

"But where from? That lane—not a road even—doesn't lead anywhere that someone like that would be coming from and it's not a shortcut."

"I know," he said. "That puzzled me. I can only imagine it wasn't a local but some visitor who'd got lost."

"At that time of day? Anyway, if, as you said, the vehicle was probably a four-by-four, possibly a Land Rover—that sounds like a local to me."

He shook his head. "Believe me," he said, "I've thought about all that, and if it wasn't an accident but a deliberate attempt to run someone down, well, there doesn't seem to be any sort of motive. At least his partner hasn't been able to come up with anything."

"I do see all that," I said, "but there might be something none of us—not even Patrick—knows about."

He smiled. "I see you want to make a mystery of it."

"Yes, I know, but this time it's sort of personal, my best friend's cousin. So you do see why I had to listen to Patrick and why I wonder too."

"I can only assure you, Mrs. Malory," he said, "that I'm keeping an open mind on the subject and if you can find anything at all that might help I'd be glad to hear it."

I rang Patrick and told him what Bob Morris had said. "At least," I said, "he's thinking about it. If only there was any sort of reason for wanting Daniel out of the way." A sudden thought struck me. "Has that farmer been onto you about taking water across the field at the cottage?"

"Yes, he has, as a matter of fact. Quite soon after the funeral. Too soon—I gave him a pretty sharp answer. Why, do you think—"

"There's quite a lot of money involved. He wants to set up some sort of super camping site with yurts, or whatever they're called, and so forth and he needs to get the water to his fields for that. And I'm sure *he* would have a Land Rover."

"But surely that wouldn't be sufficient reason for actually *killing* someone."

"I suppose not," I said reluctantly. "Well, keep on thinking—I'm sure you're right about it being deliberate and I do believe Bob Morris thinks so too."

"I think of nothing else," Patrick said wearily, "but there doesn't seem to be anything we can do."

I'd finally nerved myself to clean out my kitchen cupboards when Rosemary arrived.

"Oh dear," she said, looking at all the tins on the kitchen table, "sorry if I've arrived at a bad time."

"No, it's a perfect time," I said, cheerfully putting them back into the cupboard again. "I've been trying to decide how many of these things that are out of date I can still use. Too depressing!"

"Oh, I know—I'm sure things in tins are OK if they *look* all right. Anyway, remember Captain Scott's jam—it was years and years old when they dug it out of the snow and that was fine."

"Well," I said as I shut the cupboard door firmly,

"it's lovely to see you. I'll put the kettle on. Is it anything special or just a chat?"

"Both really—it seems ages since we got together, but, what with Mother . . . she's home now and expecting the same level of service she had in hospital. Poor Elsie's been having to cook all sorts of complicated things that Mother says she's been *so* looking forward to and I've been run off my feet looking for little delicacies she might fancy. If it wasn't for Patrick I do think I'd have gone mad!"

"He still comes round?"

"Oh yes, nearly every day. He's so good with her and encourages her to do all the exercises the physio says she must do and she won't do for me."

"Well done Patrick. He's a strange person. I still don't feel I really know him."

She thought for a moment. "No—I feel the same. He's perfectly normal, agreeable, chatty—just a polite young man, but you always feel he's holding something back. I mean, sometimes I feel he's too good to be true, especially with Mother. But then, I'm not used to anyone getting on so well with her, especially someone of such a different generation."

"Just what I feel. I did, I think, catch a glimpse of what might be the real Patrick once when he let his guard down, but, in general, he does seem to feel the need to put up this front."

"How was he with Daniel? I never really saw them together."

"Whenever I saw them he'd put on that 'front,' as

you call it. I don't know how they were in private. I do
know Eva said that Dan relied on him a lot—all the
practical things, business, daily living and so forth, but
she never said anything about their personal relations.
I suppose she felt that might seem like prying. Certainly Dan's death really seems to have got to him. I
suppose he's told you that he doesn't think it was an
accident—quite obsessive about it, but, really, what sort
of motive would anyone have for killing someone like
Dan?"

"I know."

"Anyway, I'm glad to say he seems to be settled at
the cottage; Mother would be devastated if he went
away. Which reminds me. He was quite worried about
what to do with Alan's papers. He asked me if I wanted
to have them, but really I wouldn't know what to do
with them."

"Eva said that Alan's publisher wanted to publish
some of them or to get someone to do a sort of biography appreciation. Perhaps Patrick could just send
them to him."

"That would be best." She thought for a moment.
"There's just one thing. There might be some personal
stuff there that Eva might not have wanted published.
Sheila, would you mind going through them, just to
have a look? I know how busy you are with reviews
and things but I don't think I could do it and it would
set my mind at rest."

"Yes, of course, I'd be glad to. I'd like to feel I was
doing something for Eva."

"Bless you. There's no rush. I'll tell Patrick and he can bring them over to you sometime."

"That's fine. The kettle's boiled—tea or coffee?"

Patrick brought round the papers a few days later in cardboard boxes which he nobly carried up to the spare room.

"I'm afraid there's rather a lot," he said. "I hope it's not too much for you."

"No, it's all right—I knew how much there was. Rosemary and I helped Eva carry them in from the garage after there was that fire."

"A fire?"

"Yes. Fortunately it didn't do too much damage—they caught it in time. Some sort of fault in the wiring. These must have been taking up quite a bit of room in the cottage. Eva had been going to sort them out but she never got round to it. Anyway, I'll go through them and separate the letters from the articles and scripts and take out anything personal that she wouldn't have wanted printed. Then the publisher can appoint someone to prepare the articles for press and perhaps do a critical bibliography."

"Couldn't you do that?"

"Goodness, no. It's not my field. Geoffrey Bailey—he's the publisher—probably has someone in mind."

Foss, who had been prowling round the boxes in a supervisory capacity, selected one, jumped up onto it and composed himself for sleep.

"Come and have a coffee," I said, "and possibly

some cake. You must need some sustenance after all that heavy lifting."

I led us both into the kitchen hoping that an informal atmosphere might make him more relaxed. He made a fuss of Tris, who greeted him enthusiastically and then settled down near his feet.

I got out some tins. "Sponge cake or chocolate?"

"Oh, chocolate, please. Comfort food." He smiled. "We used to have a lot of comfort food—sort of nice everyday things as a treat after all the peculiar things Dan had to eat in his job."

"Yes, I remember he asked Rosemary for the local sausages and mash when she had you both to dinner and was worried about cooking for him." I cut large slices for both of us. "What do you cook for yourself?"

"Not very much . . ." He turned his head away and I busied myself switching on the kettle and fussing with the cups.

"Don't you think it's strange," he said quietly, "Alan, then Eva and then Daniel . . . all dead?"

"It is tragic," I said, "like some Greek play, but Alan and Eva died of natural causes."

"But did they?"

"What do you mean?"

"Oh, I don't know," he said. "I suppose I'm just looking for some explanation other than a particularly cruel fate. But, think of it," he went on eagerly. "Alan managed to survive all those dangerous experiences and there *could* be something odd about Eva's death—there was no one there when she died. And then, Dan . . ."

"Yes, I know," I said, "and I do agree with you about Daniel's death—there's something really wrong there—but not the other two; it's just not possible."

"No, you're probably right—I'm just clutching at straws. It's so hard to accept."

"I know, and this business about Daniel—there are a lot of questions there—makes it even harder. I'm glad you're staying on here."

"I'm not going until I find out who killed Dan," he said.

"So you see," I said to Rosemary the next day, "it looks as though he's here for quite a while. Your mother will be pleased, but, poor boy, I really don't see how anyone can ever say how that terrible thing happened."

I was surprised to get a phone call from Bob Morris.

"I thought I'd let you know," he said. "I've just heard from Mrs. Porter—she's the elderly lady who lives in the cottage further down the lane. I did hope to interview her at the time but she's been away. Only just got back and was very shocked to hear about the accident—she'd really taken to 'the two boys,' as she called them, had them to tea and so forth. Anyway, that morning she hadn't been able to sleep and had got up to make herself a cup of tea round about the time it happened. Her kitchen faces the road and when she heard a vehicle coming she was curious to know who was about so early."

"And she saw the car?" I asked eagerly.

"She saw a Land Rover, and since it's not likely there would have been two going down that lane at that time, I think we can assume it was the one. It was quite light by then and it was going slowly so she had a good view. She said it was a Land Rover with a metal top—which sounds like a Land Rover Defender, which narrows it down a bit. It struck her as odd, someone out at that time of day, and it wasn't one she recognized—not belonging to anyone round there."

"I don't suppose she got the number?"

"I'm afraid not, but then, people don't, more's the pity. And unfortunately she couldn't see the driver. Still, it's a step forward."

"If it was going slowly," I said, "that might have been because the driver was looking out for Daniel— might have known he'd be out there running at that time. He did it nearly every day."

"Yes."

"So it must have been someone who knew him, knew about his movements."

"Exactly."

"You've told Patrick?"

"Of course. I wanted to know if he'd seen anyone about in the days before it happened."

"Someone who might have been checking Daniel's movements? And had he?"

"He said he was usually in the kitchen—theirs is at the back of the house—getting breakfast for when Daniel got back. But, of course, the person might have been waiting somewhere further down the lane—off the road, even. There's the turning that leads to the farm, quite a high hedge, and you could park in there and not be seen by anyone driving casually by."

"Oh dear—it's so frustrating. Still, you can check on all the Defenders, I suppose."

"I can if it's someone from inside the area, but it may not have been."

"But you're sure now that it wasn't an accident—was deliberate?"

"It certainly needs thinking about."

I was thinking about it as I took down the kitchen curtains to be washed. It really did look as if Daniel's death was deliberate—Bob Morris seemed much more certain now that he'd heard from Mrs. Porter. I knew her slightly and she was someone who took an interest in things and people around her, a keen observer (or just plain curious), so I was sure she would have got her facts right, and certainly Bob hadn't hesitated to accept her evidence. It was wonderful that she had been there at that particular time but so frustrating that she hadn't been able to see the driver. If it was someone local I was sure she could have identified him. Still, it *was* a step forward, especially if it convinced Bob that there really was a case to answer. I was glad there was something for Patrick to feel good about.

I balanced carefully on the small stepladder (I'm not very good on ladders) and began to unhook the curtains. It was such a pity, too, that Patrick's kitchen didn't face the road or he might have seen the car as well. It did seem possible that the driver might have stopped in that gateway, waiting for Daniel to come by. As I took the hooks out of the curtains I thought that perhaps I might take Tris for a walk along that part of the lane. I'd have to be sure that Patrick was with Mrs. Dudley—I wouldn't want him to think I was being insensitive, looking at the site of the tragedy. As I folded the curtains I suddenly decided that I really didn't like them. They had a sort of square Greek key pattern round the bottom, quite unsuitable, it now seemed to me, for a kitchen. I stuffed them in the machine to wash them before I took them to the charity shop. Then I went up to the airing cupboard to see what I could find to replace them.

Chapter Fifteen

Since Rosemary happened to mention that Patrick was going to tea with Mrs. Dudley the next day, I decided to go and have a look at the lane. I parked just before the turning to the farm, hoping that no other car would want to get by. I remembered Bob had said that, because of the dry weather, there hadn't been any useful tire marks where Daniel was killed so I wasn't very hopeful of finding anything. But, by a piece of luck, the opening of the turning was in a hollow which had held the rain that had fallen before and, although the ground was dry and baked hard, there were definite marks where it had been damp and where a vehicle had stood. I bent down to examine them and was disappointed. They were like small squares (reminding me of the pattern on my curtains) and didn't look like tire marks to me. Still, I thought I should tell Bob about them and see what he thought. I suddenly panicked that there might be heavy rain or they might be obliterated in some way before he could come and look at them, then I remembered that my mobile phone also worked as a camera.

I took it out of my bag and regarded it doubtfully. I'd never tried to use it as a camera, in spite of Michael having explained how it worked. I can only cope with very basic technology.

I switched it on and pressed things until it said menu and finally found something that looked promising. I crouched down and pressed things again, hoping that I was doing the right thing.

Back in the car I thought of using the mobile phone to tell Bob about the marks, but I was afraid of messing up the photos (if I *had* taken them) so I had to wait until I got home.

Fortunately I was able to get through to him quite quickly and told him what I'd found.

"They don't look like tire marks," I said, "but I thought I'd better let you know about them." I described what they looked like and he asked me to repeat it. He sounded quite excited.

"Were they any use?" I asked. "I think I may have been able to photograph them on my mobile, but I'm not sure."

"I'd really like to look at the photos. I have an idea of what the marks may be . . . Would it be convenient for me to come round on my way home?"

When he came I watched anxiously while he pressed things.

"Did I manage to take anything?" I asked.

He smiled. "Well, they're not exactly professional standard, but I can see quite clearly what they are. They're the marks of off-road tires."

"Is that good?"

"Not all Defenders have them, so it does narrow things down a bit more."

"And you'll go and have a look yourself?"

"Most certainly. And I've widened the search. It doesn't seem that anyone who had anything to do with Daniel has a Defender, so it may well have been hired. Of course, whoever it is may have gone further afield, but at least I can start by checking places that hire Land Rovers in the area."

"And you'll tell Patrick?"

"Of course."

After that, I thought I might have heard from Patrick, but Rosemary told me he'd had to go up to London—something about selling the flat.

"So it does look as if he's going to be staying down here," she said. "Mother's delighted."

"But what will he *do* down here?" I asked.

"I haven't the faintest idea. I'm just glad that, whatever it is he's going to do, he'll be doing it in Taviscombe. Anyway, what I really wanted to ask you is if you'd come shopping with me in Taunton. I've got to find a birthday present for Delia and I need all the help I can get to find something—anything—she might like."

It was, as I expected, a fruitless expedition and

Rosemary ended up (as I always knew she would do) buying Delia a generous Marks & Spencer token.

"More birthdayish" Rosemary said, "than actual money, and she'll have the pleasure of spending it herself. I don't know about you but I feel it's time for lunch and a nice sit-down."

"Good idea. We're near the precinct so let's go to the tearoom there; they do light lunches."

"This is nice and peaceful," Rosemary said, "after that crowded food hall. Still we did buy *something* so it wasn't quite a wasted journey and I was able to get those special cheese biscuits for Mother—no one has them in Taviscombe."

We sat for a while over our lunch, just enjoying being somewhere away from home, and the café began to fill up with lunchtime office workers.

"Look," Rosemary said, "isn't that Maurice Shelby? I think he's seen us but he's not going to join us."

I laughed. "He did join me that time over a toasted tea cake and was quite human, but I imagine the thought of having his lunch with *two* females was just too much for him."

"Just as well," she said. "He always looks so dismal. Actually, it sounds as if he has things to be dismal about. Jack says he might be struggling—not many new clients."

"I feel sorry for him. It must be so difficult for older solicitors like him these days when the whole procedure's been speeded up and everything is timed to the last second and much more impersonal. I know Michael doesn't really like it and he's adaptable, so someone like Maurice Shelby couldn't help being left behind."

"Perhaps he'll retire—he must be well over sixty—and there's always Alison's money." She looked at her watch. "If it's all right with you, we really ought to be going. Elsie's going to the dentist so I've got to give Mother her tea. Come to think of it, I might just buy her some of the gorgeous gâteau they sell here. That should cheer her up."

I'd been putting off looking at Alan's papers but the next morning, when there was nothing I really had to do, I decided to get on with it. I crouched down in the spare room, prising open one of the cardboard boxes. As I opened it and started to take out some of the papers, I was aware of a slightly acrid smell—a reminder of the smoke from the fire in Eva's garage. I took a large bundle of papers downstairs to my study and began to go through them. These were all articles that Alan had written over the years, scripts of interviews and notes for broadcasts, so I put them to one side together with those from the other boxes. Next I found a box of letters, mostly concerned with his work, though there were some from Eva, which I removed without reading and which I planned to pass on to Rosemary. There were also a few letters from well-known people that I kept separately to go in the biography. It all seemed quite straightforward and I'd made good progress by lunchtime.

Rosemary came round in the afternoon, so I was able to give her Eva's letters.

"I haven't come across any from Daniel," I said, "but there are still several boxes I haven't looked at yet."

"Daniel may not have written letters—the young mostly communicate by e-mail or even by text messages. I don't know what Eva did with Alan's laptop or his mobile. I suppose they may still be at the cottage. I'd better ask Patrick. We didn't get around to doing much in the way of clearing up when Eva died and Daniel came down to live there . . ."

"Oh well, there's no urgency, though I suppose there may be things on the laptop that might go in the biography. Did Eva ever mention it?"

"No, it was like the papers—I suppose she really didn't want to face the fact that Alan was gone."

"Well, there's not a lot left to do with them. I should finish sorting things out tomorrow and then they can go off for the publisher to deal with."

Next morning I worked hard at the boxes, opening the last one with a sense of relief. I was intrigued to find that it contained a series of notebooks containing what looked like a diary written in Alan's neat handwriting. Not an actual diary with entries for separate days, but a kind of narrative of some of his journeys. I began by skimming through it, but soon became fascinated and settled down to read it properly. It covered his work in several different countries and was written in a free, open style so that I could hear Alan's distinctive voice coming through. As I read on, I became excited about what seemed to me a most unusual and brilliant piece of work, something that really should be published. I wished Eva could have read it—Daniel too—they would have been so proud.

As the narrative moved on to South America I was startled to find Donald Webster's name leaping at me from the page. Then I remembered Eva saying that Alan had met Donald out there and he had rescued them both from some sort of tight spot. I read on eagerly, enjoying Alan's laconic account of how they'd met by chance and had found themselves caught up in a raid on a major drug dealer and how he'd managed to talk their way out of danger. All quite casual, typical of Alan, but I could see how frightening it must have been and could understand Donald's admiration of him. They each seemed to have gone their own way after that and there was no further mention of Donald until nearly the end of Alan's stay in the country.

It seems there'd been an explosion at one of the chemical factories—apparently not an unusual occurrence so there was no worldwide coverage in the press, although a number of workers had been killed. There was an investigation and, from the information given, it was pronounced to be an accident. But Alan, with his reporter's instinct, was not satisfied, and from the contacts he'd made, he was sure that it had been the result of negligence on the part of the company. There was no actual evidence and many of the people involved wouldn't talk to him for fear of losing their jobs with the company. But the general feeling was that Donald Webster, as the person in charge, had been aware of the situation that led to the explosion and had, presumably for financial reasons, done nothing about it.

I stared at the page until the handwriting became blurred. Then I read on. Alan didn't want to let go, but, reluctantly, finally decided that with no evidence or confirmed witness statement there was nothing he could do. He made some very forthright comments about Donald Webster, who had, by then, been transferred to another country—actually, another continent.

I sat for some time considering what to do. Finally I decided to show Rosemary the notebook.

She came round quickly when I said it was something urgent and I sat her down and found her the entry. Like me, she was stunned. Finally she said, "I never thought I'd say this, but I'm glad Eva died when she did. For heaven's sake," she said fiercely, "she might have married him and then it all could have come out. How would she have felt then!"

"This explains why he was so keen to 'help' look through the papers," I said. "He knew Alan had been in the area and was afraid he might have written something. Which, thank God, he did!"

"I always thought there was something wrong about that man—you remember, I never trusted him and was sure he'd hurt Eva in some way."

"You were certainly right about that," I said. "He fooled everybody—still does. When I think how sorry I was for him when he seemed so upset about her death!"

"For all we know, it might have been just an act—all that with Eva—just to get hold of the papers."

"I think he was genuinely attracted to her," I said reluctantly. "Oh, I don't know—how can you tell with someone like that?"

We sat for a moment in silence, then Rosemary said suddenly, "The fire! Was that him? Did *he* start it deliberately? Eva could have been killed in that fire—did he think of that!"

"It could have been deliberate—I think we just assumed it was faulty wiring." I thought for a moment. "When Eva died he must have thought he was safe."

"He offered to help sort out the papers after she died. I'd have been glad to accept the offer—there was so much to see to, but, fortunately, I was so upset I couldn't be bothered with them just then."

"He offered again when Daniel died," I said. "But then there was Patrick . . ."

We sat in silence again for some minutes.

"What are we going to do?" I asked. "Whatever we feel like, I don't imagine there's any way anyone could bring him to justice."

"We must confront him," Rosemary said. "Tell him that we know what he's done."

"I don't know that I could bear to look at him," I said.

"Well *I* certainly can and I'll tell everyone in Taviscombe what a loathsome person he is."

"He'll deny it, of course."

"But we've got Alan's notebook," Rosemary said.

"Yes, but *he* said there was no evidence so nothing

could be done. We could be sued for libel or defamation or something."

"That's ridiculous!"

"But I'm right. Jack will tell you so."

"We can't let him get away with it."

"No, I agree, but all we can do is to let him know *we* know and that Alan described the whole affair—we needn't go into details, just hint that there's some damning stuff there. Frighten him."

"Then what?"

"Then he'll probably go away."

"And get off scot-free?"

"I know that seems unfair, but he'd never know for sure if we might produce something positive against him."

"But can't we tell the police?"

"There's nothing they can do without the real facts—and, anyway, it happened in another country so they couldn't do anything anyway."

"It's so frustrating. Will you come with me to see him?"

"Yes, of course I will. Where shall we see him?"

"We could confront him at Brunswick Lodge, then everyone would know."

"Libel!"

"Oh, I suppose so."

"I'll invite him round here. He's been here for tea before so he won't be suspicious and put us off, though I won't tell him you'll be here—that might surprise him and throw him off balance a bit."

I telephoned and invited him round ("for coffee") and he arranged to come the next day.

He was a little surprised to find Rosemary, but greeted her in his usual easy manner.

"We've invited you here," I said, "because of a very important matter."

"That sounds serious," he said lightly.

"It is, very serious. As you know, Alan left a lot of papers, mostly connected with his work. You do know that, of course, because you offered your help in going through them."

His attitude was very wary now but he said, "Yes, I gather that Eva was thinking of getting them published. I'm sure any publisher would want them—they must be most interesting."

"I certainly found them so," I said, "when I went through them."

"You did?"

"Yesterday. Which is why I asked you to come here today." He didn't speak so I went on. "In addition to all his professional papers he also kept a sort of journal of his travels, including an account of his time in South America. You met him there, I believe."

"Yes. He got us out of a really tight spot—I told Eva about it."

"I remember her telling me. But, what you didn't tell Eva was your connection with the explosion at that chemical factory. Alan had quite a lot to say about that in his journal."

He was silent for a moment, then he said steadily,

"That was a long time ago and I was completely exonerated of any blame. It was a very distressing incident—people were killed. I didn't tell Eva because I didn't want to upset her."

"People were killed," I said, "and it was very distressing. For them and for their families. Alan found it distressing too. If you remember, he was a reporter, someone who instinctively investigated things—you don't imagine he would have let go of something like that."

Chapter Sixteen

"I can't imagine what he thought he'd found," Donald said easily. "There was a very full inquiry, there was no evidence of mismanagement, and, as I said, I was completely cleared of any blame for what was a very distressing incident."

I could see that Rosemary was longing to let fly so I said quickly, "There was no evidence because people were afraid to say anything that might cause them to lose their jobs. But they were willing to talk to Alan."

"In such circumstances people will always look for someone to blame. I suppose I was an obvious target—there is always a lot of jealousy at certain levels. I'm sorry Alan was misled."

He paused for a moment and then he went on, " I don't know what he may have written in this journal, but I can assure you that I have done nothing wrong."

"But when you knew about the papers," Rosemary burst out, "you were worried there might be something in them that would expose you—that's why you were so anxious to 'help' with them!"

He smiled. "I was merely trying to give Eva a hand with something she obviously found difficult to do—understandably so."

"And I suppose," Rosemary said fiercely, "you had nothing to do with the fire in the garage—a fire that should have destroyed them and might have killed Eva!"

"Now you're being ridiculous," he said angrily. "I don't know what you think you're going to do with this precious journal, but if you're going to go about making accusations like that then I'll have to give instructions to my solicitor."

"And what about Eva?" Rosemary was unstoppable now. "Did you think that by marrying her you could get at the papers and destroy them?"

"That is an unforgivable thing to say," he said, tight-lipped. "I loved Eva and she loved me—I was desolated when she died."

"That's easy enough to say now she's dead," Rosemary persisted. "What do you think she'd have said if she'd known what you'd done? What do you imagine everyone will think when they know?"

"I've already warned you not to make libelous statements—" he began.

"Oh, in a place like Taviscombe," Rosemary said, "you don't have to spell things out. Just the hint that

there's something not quite right with somebody—
that's enough."

"I think what Rosemary means," I said, "is that it
would be better if you left. As you say, there's no hard
evidence about what you did, but there's enough in
Alan's journals to convince us that Taviscombe would
be a better place without you."

He got up. "There's no reason why I should stay
here and listen to this nonsense and, as for leaving
Taviscombe, I will not be blackmailed in this way. I
will do as I think fit. I have nothing more to say to
you on this matter."

He went away and as the door slammed behind
him, Rosemary said, "Do you think he will go? I'd
really like to have done *something* to make him pay
for what he did."

"So would I, but I'm afraid there's nothing we can
actually do. But I think he will leave Taviscombe—
that was a good remark of yours about hinting. And
he still doesn't know exactly what Alan wrote—I don't
think he'd want to risk it."

Rosemary sighed. "You're right, of course, but I do
feel frustrated—for Eva's sake as much as for anything else. Just think what might have happened."

I was not surprised that when I next went to Brunswick Lodge, I heard Anthea bewailing the loss of
such a useful committee member.

"He was invaluable in such a lot of ways," she was
saying to Alison Shelby. "I really don't know what

we'll do without him. And I never got him to give that second talk—it would have been so interesting, and we made such a nice lot of money from his first one."

"Why is he leaving, then?" Alison asked. "He only just got here!"

"Oh, something to do with business, I believe—I didn't get the details."

"I thought he'd retired."

"Oh no, he was in a very important position with his firm and they needed him as a consultant, or whatever they call it. I think he's got to go abroad. Anyway, he's put that lovely house on the market. Such a shame; it had a really big garden and I was hoping we could have a garden party there to raise funds for the wiring here—it's turning out to be more expensive than we thought and Derek is being so difficult about it all."

Further speculation about Donald Webster's departure was lost in Anthea's endless complaints about Derek's intransigence.

Rosemary and I decided not to tell Mrs. Dudley anything that had happened. We knew how much it would upset her. But she was less easy to satisfy. "It is the most extraordinary thing," she said to me when I went to tea. "He'd settled here so well. Such a popular man, so well thought of. I was not sure at first about his involvement with poor Eva, but they did seem to be fond of each other. He was absolutely devastated when she died. I remember him coming to see me shortly after that. He and I got on so well; I like to think that he turned to me at a time like that. I said what I could to comfort him, but these things go very deep with a sensitive person like that."

I made a suitable murmur.

"I must say," she said, "I was surprised that he didn't see fit to come and say good-bye to me. *Not* a very gentlemanly way to behave. I am most disappointed in him. After all," she continued with increased vigor, "I did introduce him to the best Taviscombe society and I might have expected some sort of consideration in return. There he is, gone, and no one seems to know *where*." This seemed to be a major cause for complaint. Or," she said, "why. What possible reason could he have had to leave when there was everything he could possibly want here?"

"Perhaps it was something to do with his job," I suggested.

"That's as may be, but it is no reason to go off like that without a word to people who have done their best to make him feel at home in Taviscombe. I have had him to tea here—and lunch too—and made him welcome in my home and I do resent being treated in such a way."

"Oh well," Rosemary said when I told her about Mrs. Dudley's reaction. "It's best that she should be angry with him for his lack of politeness than for the real reason. That would really be too much for her."

"Absolutely."

Rosemary laughed. "She actually said that *I* was always prejudiced against him—the nearest she could get to admitting that she was wrong and I was right. Oh well, she'll get over it. Thank goodness she's got Patrick to occupy her. He still comes quite often. She's getting him to go on working on that family tree that Eva started. Apparently Daniel was going to do something about it before . . ."

"I think that would be a good thing," I said. "Another shared interest for them. And it's something he can feel he's doing for Daniel."

"Eva's laptop is still at the cottage," Patrick said when I saw him next, "and Rosemary said it would be all right for me to use it because it has the genealogy stuff on it. There's not much. Eva had only just made a start, and Daniel—Daniel didn't have time to do much to it."

"Is it difficult to trace things?" I asked. "I've always wanted to look up my family, and Peter's, but there seemed to be so many things to wade through."

"It's a bit tedious, going through all the census entries, but I'm getting the hang of it."

"Well do keep up the good work—it means a lot to Mrs. Dudley."

"I try to report back to her," he said. "I think it helps her, just talking about them all. Not that she knows much about Eva's immediate family, but she's got quite a lot to say about some of the more distant relations on her husband's side of the family."

I laughed. "I bet she has!"

"Actually," Patrick went on, "there's quite a lot of Eva's things still at the cottage. Rosemary more or less left things as they were when Dan came down and I'm not sure what she wants done with them. I haven't really liked to ask her . . ."

"No, of course you haven't. I'll have a word with her, shall I?"

"Thank you. That would be best." There was a silence for a minute then he said, "I believe Donald Webster has gone away. Do you know if he's coming back?"

"I wouldn't think so. Why do you ask?"

"Just the other day I came across a book of his— at least it had his name written in it—and I ought to get it back to him."

"I suppose he must have lent it to Eva," I said. "What was the book?"

"Some sort of travel book, about South America. What shall I do with it?"

"Oh, put it with the other books. I don't think anyone knows where he's gone, so you can't return it."

Donald Webster's sudden departure was something of a nine days' wonder but was swiftly overtaken by an escalation of the disagreement between Anthea and Derek over the rewiring. Sides were being taken (and umbrage) and such an atmosphere of hostility existed that several of the more sensitive members avoided Brunswick Lodge altogether.

"I wonder where he's gone," Rosemary said. "Putting his house on the market was pretty final."

"The general opinion favors abroad," I replied, "and

I expect that's the most likely—*not* back to South America, though. Anyway, the main thing is he's gone and I know you feel he shouldn't have got away with things, but I think it's better in the end."

"I suppose so."

"Oh, by the way, Patrick was wondering what you wanted to do about Eva's things at the cottage. He didn't like to approach you directly; I think he felt it might be painful for you to decide."

"Well, I did rather put things off after she died and then it seemed all right to leave things as they were when Daniel was there. But now—I don't know. I suppose I must do something now that Daniel's left the cottage to Patrick. He did ask me about the laptop, and of course I did say go on using it, but there's a lot of other stuff, even though we took Alan's papers away. Oh dear, I really don't know what to do."

"I don't think Patrick's in any hurry," I said. "I'm sure he's happy to leave things as they are until you've had a little think."

"It's all been such a mess, one thing after another— first Alan, then Eva, then Daniel! I suppose I really ought to ask Mother what she thinks, but I expect she won't want me to do anything that might upset Patrick and make him go away."

Rosemary's words about one thing after another stayed with me and somehow nagged away until I confronted them. It *was* an unusual set of circumstances, the three of them going so suddenly and in such a short space of time. Alan's death, I accepted, was simply from natural causes and so, in a way was Eva's. And yet there was something different about that. She died suddenly and alone and, although there appeared to be a perfectly understandable medical reason for it, I still felt uneasy. Possibly it was guilt, because I hadn't been able to do anything at the time, but somehow I felt it wasn't just that. Not with Daniel's unexplained death coming so soon after. That was not a tragic accident, but something deliberate, and if that was deliberate, what about Eva's death? Could that, somehow, have been arranged? But how and why?

I tried to put it out of my mind and didn't even tell Rosemary what I was thinking. I was quite busy just then, because Thea had a gastric upset and I was taking Alice back and forth to school and feeding her and making the odd casserole for Michael and I had enough to do just keeping up with things, not to mention the animals who, as usual, resented my attention given to anyone but them. However, when I was in the chemist collecting a prescription for Thea, something occurred to me. It was a very tentative idea and I put it to one side until I could examine it properly.

When I got home I sat down with a cup of tea and tried to concentrate. Being in the chemist had reminded me of an occasion when I'd been given the wrong prescription. That had been at a very busy time when there was a long queue of people waiting and too few assistants to deal with them. They'd been short-staffed for quite a while and things did sometimes get a bit chaotic. I'd taken back the wrong prescription and got the right one, but they were too busy to do more than give me a hasty apology. I hadn't thought much of it at the time, just accepting, as you do, that things were difficult for them. But now it occurred to me that, for someone with something more sinister in mind, it might have been the perfect opportunity to tamper with someone else's medication.

If that person had gone in at a busy time (and it was perfectly possible to calculate when things would be at their worst) and said they were collecting Eva's prescription for her, as I'd just collected one for Thea, it wouldn't have been queried but they would have simply handed it over. Then that person could have taken it home, very carefully undone the packaging, opened the box of syringes and tampered with them in some way, perhaps substituting sterile water for the insulin. Then doing up the packaging, the person could have taken it back (at an equally busy time) and exchanged it for his or her own prescription with no questions asked. It was most unlikely that any of the assistants would have remembered an incident that happened only too frequently. When Eva collected her prescription, she would have had no idea that the contents had been interfered with.

It was possible. Certain things would have been necessary. The person must have known Eva well enough to know when she collected her prescription (usually monthly, like me), would have to have had a prescription themselves or to have been in the habit of collecting one for someone else, and had to have known about the possibility of confusion at certain times of day. It could have been done.

Eva would have used the syringes, expecting them to contain insulin, then, when she got that virus, even if she'd been in a state to go on using them, they would have had no effect. The fact of the virus giving a reason for her not to take her insulin was a piece of luck for the killer. It all fitted in. It was all very complicated and, even, far-fetched and what reason would anyone have for killing Eva? The only person who had anything like a motive was Donald Webster. He was away at the time of her death and if he'd tampered with the medication he had the opportunity to give himself the perfect alibi. Would he really have gone that far? If Rosemary had been right in accusing him of putting Eva's life in danger when (if) he set fire to the garage, then I suppose the idea of killing Eva by some other means might have been possible. But it seemed a terrible step to take to get his hands on some papers that just might have contained references to his actions in South America.

Then there was Daniel's death. Donald Webster must, of course, have known of the existence of Daniel, but he may not have known much about his lifestyle. Eva may have given him the impression that Daniel was wholly tied up with his life and work in London; he wouldn't have considered the possibility of his actually living in the cottage. When he did so and with the papers still there, he too was a threat. Certainly I could make out a case of sorts against Donald Webster but was I just getting carried away with what was, after all, a pretty unlikely idea? Then I remembered that on the day I was given the wrong prescription I'd run into

him on my way out of the chemist and told him what
had happened. And then, I also remembered, that
when I'd launched into a description of what had
happened, he'd changed the subject quite abruptly.

Unlikely as it might seem, it *was* possible that he
had killed both Eva and Daniel. Certainly I could think
of no one else with any sort of motive for doing so.
And Rosemary and I had sent him away; nobody knew
where, so, if he was the killer there was probably no
way of finding him.

Chapter Seventeen

I didn't tell Rosemary or Patrick about my theory. Whether it was right or wrong it would upset them, and if I told Bob Morris he would give me one of his quizzical looks and say that it was an interesting idea. I got on with my life, only occasionally taking the theory out and thinking about it, but coming to no conclusion. Finally I decided that, even if it was true, there was nothing anyone could do about it now.

Meanwhile, the atmosphere at Brunswick Lodge had simmered down enough for us to have a reasonably peaceful discussion about the forthcoming bring-and-buy sale. Anthea had won the battle, of course, by her usual method of simply tanking over the opposition and taking it for granted that everything had been settled to her satisfaction.

"So, Sheila, what can we expect from you?" she asked me briskly, pen poised over the notebook she had taken to using on such occasions, obviously feeling that if the promises had been actually written down there was less likelihood of backsliding.

"Oh," I said firmly, "I can't manage to bring anything this time, but I'll come and buy, of course."

Naturally I wasn't getting away with that. Anthea questioned me closely, but for once I stayed firm. "Well, if you can't," she said grudgingly, "I suppose we must manage as best we can." She turned to Alison Shelby, who'd just come in. "Now, then, what shall I put you down for?"

"Oh dear, I really don't know if I can manage anything this time. Maurice has to be away for a few days and there's always such a lot to do when he's not here to help."

Having been balked of one victim, Anthea was not going to allow another to escape. She assumed the wheedling tone that sometimes produced results. "I'm sure you could whip up a batch of those splendid scones, or one of your sponges—they always go well."

Flattered by this attention, Alison hesitated for a fatal moment. "Well, I suppose I could just make a sponge and I suppose the scones—though those ought to be made on the day unless I make them earlier and freeze them . . ."

I slipped away while Anthea was occupied and took refuge in the Buttery, where I was joined by Rosemary, who was looking harassed.

"I'm absolutely exhausted," she said, putting down

her tray with some violence. "I've been trying to find some Gentleman's Relish for Mother. Apparently Patrick has never heard of it and Mother's determined that he shall try some. Of course, none of the supermarkets have any, nor the farm shop, nor the deli. It looks as if I'll have to go to Taunton for it."

"I suppose you could make some," I suggested, "with anchovies and butter."

"No use, it has to be in one of those special jars with Patum Peperium on the label. Nothing else will do."

"Oh dear."

"Of course I'm delighted that she's taken to Patrick—it's helped so much since Daniel died. But I'm really nervous—suppose he suddenly takes it into his head to go off somewhere."

"I think he's pretty well settled, at least for the moment," I said consolingly.

"So he says, but you never know with the young, and, as we've always said, we really know nothing about him."

"I'm sure it will be all right."

"Oh well," Rosemary said resignedly, "I suppose I'd better enjoy it while it lasts, even if it does mean combing Taunton for a jar of Gentleman's Relish."

Patrick came to coffee a few mornings later. To my surprise he'd taken to accepting my invitations—just coming for coffee to keep it casual, though I was hoping to work up to tea or even supper. This time he'd brought with him some of the genealogical stuff he'd got off the Internet.

"I think I'm getting the hang of it," he said, "making some progress, and working backward. I'm concentrating on Eva's family—that's the one Mrs. Dudley's interested in, of course—I've got as far as her parents. It's tricky getting the Australian stuff, but, as he died in England I got enough from the death certificate to help me. He was a Benson and her maiden name was Castel, which is unusual and should help."

"Yes, I remember Eva mentioning it—I think she said that family came from the other side of the county."

"You don't remember where, do you? It would help with the census things."

"She said nearly in Dorset, but that's not a lot of use, I'm afraid."

"Oh well, I'll try all the possible larger towns and see if I can come up with something. This is what I've got so far." He took a lot of papers from a folder and I stared at them dutifully but, really, couldn't make much sense of any of it, finding the printouts of the various census returns extremely difficult to read. However, I made encouraging noises and he gathered them up, promising to let me know how he'd got on.

"I'd better go," he said. "I'd like to get a bit more done—I've been invited to tea with Mrs. Dudley this afternoon. I had hoped to carry on with this but she seemed particularly anxious for me to go today."

"Ah, yes. Do you like anchovies?" I asked.

He looked at me inquiringly. "As a matter of fact I do."

"Thank goodness for that," I said.

* * *

Reluctantly I decided that I was due to put the antiflea stuff on Tris and Foss. It's something you really need two people for—one to hold the animal still and one to open the awkward little vial and actually apply it. Cautiously I tempted Tris into the kitchen and shut the door, knowing that if Foss knew what I was doing he would disappear. Fortunately Tris is mostly cooperative and I held him steady with one hand and tried to part the long fur on his neck so that I could put the lotion on the actual skin but, as usual, most of it went onto the fur. Hoping that would be enough I let him go and went in search of Foss. He was in the sitting room on the sofa and I thought I'd got him cornered, but, just at that moment, Tris came in shaking himself so that it was very obvious to an intelligent Siamese what was going on. Foss was off the sofa and up the stairs before I realized what was happening, and I knew that he would already be making himself inaccessible under the spare room bed. I was just deciding whether it was worthwhile making an attempt to fetch him when the phone rang. It was Bob Morris.

"I thought you'd like to know that I think we've found the place the Defender came from. It's in Bristol and I'm going to check it out myself in case I can get a description of the person who hired it."

"That's fantastic!" I exclaimed. "And the dates fit?"

"Yes. It looks promising. I'll go down there tomorrow and let you know what I find out."

"Can I tell Patrick?"

"I'd rather you didn't—if it turns out not to be anything to do with the case, then there are privacy considerations."

"Of course. I quite understand. Well—good luck!"

I put the phone down and wandered around the house in a state of excitement. It seemed almost too good to be true. Bob had done a splendid job and it looked as though we were at least one step nearer finding out who had killed Daniel. Foss, erroneously thinking it was safe to reappear, strolled downstairs. Still buoyant from the excitement of the telephone call, I scooped him up, put him on the worktop in the kitchen and put the flea stuff on him all in one moment of triumph.

I'd promised Thea that I'd collect Alice's new school blazer from the shop in Taunton, and I thought I'd better get it done while I actually had a free day. It was a tiresome drive—the inadequate road from Taviscombe to Taunton was cluttered up with heavy lorries and, since there are virtually no passing places, there were endless queues, and the rain made it all the more frustrating. When I finally got there I had to wait, anxiously and illegally parked on a yellow line, while they sorted through the newly arrived stock to find what I wanted. By then it was past lunchtime so I went, as I usually do, to find something to eat in the tea shop in the precinct. I'd just relaxed with coffee and a toasted sandwich when, to my horror, I saw Alison Shelby surveying the tables. I hastily turned my head away, but I was too late.

"Fancy seeing you here," she said, putting her tray down and sitting down comfortably opposite to me. "What a nice surprise."

I gave her a wintry smile. "I like to come here when I'm in Taunton," I said. "It's usually nice and peaceful."

"Yes, isn't it!" she said enthusiastically. "Maurice comes here sometimes—it's quite near his office—and he always speaks so well of it. So what are you doing so far from home?"

Swallowing my irritation at this form of address, I explained the purpose of my errand, which, alas, set her off on the wicked expense of school uniforms and how many "extras" private schools expected the parents to buy. I tried to let the flow of language wash over me.

"Unfortunately the girls went to different schools, boarding schools of course—there's nothing suitable round here. Lydia was always the brainy one so she needed somewhere academic, while Charlotte was a very *practical* girl, so we found a very nice place in Switzerland, more of a finishing school, really. Of course, it cost the earth, but you do like to do the best you can for your children, don't you?"

I agreed that you did.

"But unfortunately it doesn't stop there, not with girls." She poured herself another cup of tea. "They both married well, I'm glad to say—such a relief when you see the sort of young person some parents are faced with. Both professional men and both doing very well. But weddings are *so* expensive—at least, if they're done properly. I said to Maurice that we owed it to the girls to put on a good show, especially since their husbands' families were—well, you know, of a certain class."

I made some sort of noncommittal noise and she ate a forkful of her gâteau and, thus refreshed, started off on a new tack.

"I'm sure I'm not one to complain," she said, "but I do think Anthea was a little *demanding* about the bring-and-buy sale. I'm quite willing to do my bit, but I did explain that Maurice was going to be away just then—he sometimes has to go away, visiting clients and so forth—and there's always a lot extra to do when you're on your own. I'm sure you must find that, situated as you are—and, out in the country, it's especially difficult."

"Yes," I said gathering my things together, "Anthea can be a little overpowering at times. But I really must be going. I have to collect Alice from school."

"What it is to be a grandmother! Alas, we have no grandchildren as yet; the young seem to lead such busy lives," she said wistfully, "but I suppose there's plenty of time yet."

A few days later Patrick came to coffee again.

"How was the Gentleman's Relish?" I asked.

"Oh, was that what you meant when you were asking about anchovies? I loved it."

"Thank goodness for that."

He looked a little puzzled but took some papers out of a folder and spread them out on the table. "I've managed to track down quite a bit of the family and made a sort of family tree. Here we are." He spread out a large sheet of paper and began to read. "Now this is Eva's great-grandfather William Benson, and he married Sarah Eliot (I think that's where the connection with Rosemary's branch of the family comes in, but I haven't traced that yet) and they had two children, James and Martha. This is where it became a bit tricky because James left England and went to Australia—I worked this out by going backward from Richard. Anyway, he married an Ellen Montgomery and their son was Richard, who came to England and married Lydia Castel and they, of course, were Eva's parents."

"So Eva had some other relations in England that she didn't know about?"

"Yes, Martha married a John Shelby and they had a son, Arthur, who married someone called Charlotte Townsend and they had a son . . ."

"Called Maurice."

Patrick looked up. "How did you know?"

I took up the paper. "Here, let me see. Yes, it must be him—the dates are right." I laid the paper down again. "What on earth is going on?"

"What do you mean?"

I tried to gather my thoughts. "Maurice Shelby," I said, "is a member of Brunswick Lodge. He knew Eva and, to my certain knowledge, talked to her about her family name, Benson, also her parents. She even

mentioned Lydia Castel—an unusual name as everyone said at the time—and he never admitted his connection with the family. In fact, he more or less denied
knowing any of the names. And he obviously knew
about the connection, even giving his daughters family Christian names."

"But why?"

"That is the question. I think I'd like to get Bill
Morris's opinion on that."

"You think there's some connection with Dan's
death?"

"I don't know, but I do feel that if we were to investigate all this further"—I indicated the family tree—
"we might just discover a motive."

"But he didn't know Dan, did he? From what you
say, he barely knew Eva, so how could he have known
about Dan's movements—how would he have known
about the running? It doesn't make sense."

"I know." I tried to think, then suddenly it occurred
to me. "Of course," I said. "Alison Shelby! His wife.
She's a tremendous gossip, always at Brunswick Lodge
listening to people's conversation, and of *course* she
would have gathered all sorts of information, quite
innocently, which she would have passed on to her
husband. She's the sort of person who never stops
talking and, although, after all these years, Maurice
Shelby must have managed to tune out all the chat, I
bet he pricked up his ears whenever she mentioned
Eva or Daniel. In fact, he probably encouraged her."

"I suppose it's possible," Patrick said.

"I've just remembered," I went on, "Alison Shelby

was standing just behind me—she had some books for Brunswick Lodge—when I was talking to Rosemary about Daniel running early in the morning."

"It's possible, I suppose."

"And another thing. I told Maurice Shelby that Daniel was tracing his family on the Internet. If there's some sort of motive in this family tree . . . Oh dear, what have I done!"

"You weren't to know. But *can* it be true?"

"I don't know, but whatever all this genealogy is about, it's the nearest thing we have to any sort of motive. What we need to know now is what Bob Morris has found out about the hire of the Land Rover in Bristol."

We didn't have long to wait. He phoned the next day. "It was the right place. The girl who dealt with it remembered him very well because he didn't look the sort of person who'd want a Land Rover. Middle-aged, with rimless spectacles, with rather a stiff manner, she said, a bit old-fashioned-looking. He had to produce his driving license, of course, and the name on it was Martin Rogers."

Chapter Eighteen

"Martin Rogers?" I said, bewildered, and I told him what Patrick and I had discovered from the family tree. "There has to be a motive somewhere there and it *has* to be Maurice Shelby who hired the car. The description fits him exactly."

Bob was definitely excited by what we'd discovered and all the other things that seemed to point to Shelby.

"That's really interesting. I'm sure you're right about him and everything I've found out does seem to reinforce what you've just told me," he said. "And, of course, he wouldn't have used his own driving license—he must have acquired this other one somehow. Anyhow, the dates are right and the mileage— from Bristol to Taviscombe and back and a bit over.

He had the Land Rover for two days so he may have stayed somewhere overnight, although he might have slept in it to make sure of being up really early." He paused. "But we had one wonderful piece of luck. No one else has hired that particular vehicle since he had it."

"So?"

"The force down there has been very cooperative and sent a forensic team to examine it and they found shreds of clothing caught up in the edge of the front bumper, just where it must have struck Daniel Jackson."

"Fantastic!"

"They also found that the steering wheel, gear lever and door handles had been wiped clean."

"That's good?"

"A bit too clever. He wore leather driving gloves—the girl remembers that because, again, they seemed so out of character. *But* he took them off when he signed the forms. I've taken all the pens he may have used and we just might be able to get something from them."

"That's amazing," I said. "Wonderful progress!"

"I think," Bob said cautiously, "we can establish that vehicle was the one that killed Daniel Jackson and that Maurice Shelby does seem to be the person who was driving it. I'm pretty sure the girl would be able to identify him."

"So what happens now?"

"Unfortunately, apart from the shreds of clothing, I wish we had more actual evidence. And a really solid motive would be nice!"

"The old detective story questions," I said. "We have How and Who, but we don't know Why."

"More or less. Perhaps a little more work on the genealogy might help."

"I can tell Patrick, then, what you've found out?"

"If you're sure he can be relied on."

"Patrick is very good at keeping secrets," I said.

I found it hard to keep all this information to myself, though it did help to be able to discuss things with Patrick, who threw himself even more enthusiastically into his genealogical searches. Still, after a few days, I managed to get more or less back to normal and was able to take an interest in the extension Michael and Thea were having made to their house.

"It means," Michael said, "we can enlarge the kitchen—it's always been a bit small for the size of the house—and make it into a kitchen-diner, and then I can have the dining room as a study instead of that dismal little box room upstairs."

"It sounds splendid," I agreed.

"And I have to do more stuff at home, at present." Michael has just been made one of the senior partners. "Actually there's a lot to do after Mrs. Armstrong's death. She didn't have any relatives so there's all her papers and documents to go through and it's easier to sort things at home rather than in the office—I'll be able to spread myself out more there. Anyway, Thea says could you possibly collect Alice from school tomorrow and give her tea because they're doing something to the floor in the kitchen then and she won't be able to get at the cooker."

So life went on, though, always at the back of my mind, was the thought of Maurice Shelby and if and why he could have possibly been a murderer. The name Martin Rogers also bothered me. It sounded somehow familiar but I couldn't place it until, when I was reading *The Free Press* and glancing at the obituary column, I suddenly remembered seeing the name there a few weeks back. So after the next committee meeting at Brunswick Lodge I asked Matthew Paisley (who seemed the most likely person to help) if he knew Martin Rogers.

"Poor old Martin. Yes, we've known him for ages and, after Joan, his wife, died—she and Marjorie were friends for years—we felt sorry for him (he'd taken it very badly) so we had him to meals and things and tried to cheer him up. But he never really got over it. Such a pity there were no children; in fact, I don't believe he had any relatives. Very sad."

"Of course, I remember him now. It's just that the name was familiar and I couldn't place him. I don't think he was one of Michael's clients . . ."

"No, Maurice Shelby was his solicitor. I always thought he was a bit old-fashioned, but Martin swore by him. Though, I suppose it suited Martin, who was a bit old-fashioned too."

Anthea, who could never bear to see two committee members in conversation without her, came up to bully one of us into acting as a steward at the next coffee morning.

"So you see," I said to Bob Morris, when I phoned him in great excitement, "that's how he got the driving license. Because Martin Rogers had no relatives, as his solicitor he'd have had access to all the documents, including the driving license. I suppose it would be too much to hope that he'd kept it after having used it in Bristol."

"It would have been very foolish of him to have done so, but people are foolish."

"Yes, that's true, and, in a way, it's the sort of thing he just might have done. An old-fashioned reluctance to destroy a document of one of his clients."

"It would be a useful piece of evidence," Bob said ruefully, "something we're painfully short of. No further genealogical stuff, I suppose?"

"Not so far. Patrick is rather handicapped by not being able to get anything new about the Australian side of the family. I wish I could remember more about Eva's father, but I didn't see much of her parents. I suppose I could ask Rosemary."

But Rosemary's memories were no more useful than mine.

"You know how it is—you never think about people of another generation—so no, I don't remember hearing him talk much about Australia. Why do you want to know?"

"I suppose it's because of Patrick doing all this family tree stuff."

I felt really bad about not being able to tell Rosemary what was going on—we always tell each other everything and I knew she'd never say anything, but I had promised Bob to keep silent. It was a nuisance that Rosemary was no more use than I was. And then I thought of someone who was far more likely than either of us to be helpful. I just needed an excuse to go and see Mrs. Dudley, quite casually, on the spur of the moment.

Fortunately I was at Brunswick Lodge when I heard Maureen complaining about having to deliver some of the parish magazines and I offered to do them for her. A perfect excuse for visiting Mrs. Dudley. I called just before eleven, pretty sure she'd ask me to stay for coffee.

"Well, this is a pleasure," Mrs. Dudley said, regarding me critically as I poured the coffee from the ornate coffee pot. "I never seem to see a single soul—everyone is so busy nowadays." Since Rosemary calls on her mother every day, this was a little unfair. "Even Patrick, dear boy, has deserted me. He's been looking up Eva's family tree on that World Wide Web, or whatever it is, and I'm very interested to know how he has been getting on."

"I believe it is very complicated," I said placatingly, "and, of course, there is the problem of the Australian connection."

"Oh, Australia," said Mrs. Dudley dismissively, annihilating the whole continent. "Though I must say for Richard, you would never have known he was a colonial—quite the gentleman and, of course, he didn't have that dreadful accent. I was a little doubtful when Edward met him and found that we had some slight connection—something to do with Edward's grandmother." Edward was Mrs. Dudley's husband, whom she referred to very rarely and then usually to back up some opinion of her own. He had died quite young (Rosemary was still at school) and somehow, since she had been a widow for so long, one never thought of her as having been a wife. "Lydia's parents were very doubtful about the marriage—well, she was an only child and there was quite a lot of money, but he was very charming and it worked out well in the end."

"Did he talk much about his life in Australia, about his parents and so forth?" I asked.

"I believe there had been some dreadful *rift* in the family," she said with relish. "His father had quarreled bitterly with *his* father—Richard's grandfather, that is—and had cut off all ties. The family in England didn't even know where he was—they'd no idea he'd gone to Australia. He never talked about it. Richard only heard about the English connection from his mother, who sounds like a sensible woman, even though she was an Australian. She didn't know much but she did tell him that the family came from near Porlock and I don't think she was surprised that he finally settled down here, though I believe his father was upset and more or less washed his hands of him."

"How sad."

"Well, he sounds like a thoroughly unpleasant man," Mrs. Dudley said firmly, "leaving his family like that and going off to the other end of the world. I always say that family is the most important thing in a person's life and not to be cast aside lightly. I have no patience with families that are always quarreling," she declared, ignoring the fact that she had, herself, cherished several long-term family feuds.

"Was Richard's father an only child?" I asked.

"That I don't know—as I said, he never spoke of his family."

"So there might be relations down here that Eva knew nothing about?"

"I suppose there might be, though I would hesitate to pursue the connection—one has no idea what sort of people they might be."

I wondered how Mrs. Dudley would consider Maurice Shelby as a family connection if our suspicions about him turned out to be true.

"I've been meaning to go up to the graves," Rosemary said, "but what with Mother's illness and everything else I haven't got around to it. I feel really badly that I've neglected them. I know the grass is cut, but they might need tidying up."

"I'll have a look at them for you," I said. "I've been meaning to clean Peter's stone for ages."

I was pleased to see that Daniel's grave had now been grassed over, as Eva's was. I pulled out a few weeds that had sprung up and went over to where Peter was buried. The church is built on a hill (as many

Somerset churches are) and his grave commands a panoramic view of the countryside he loved—the meadows below with the high moorland in the background. A beautiful spot, where, one day, I will lie beside him. I cleaned the lichen from the stone and then made my way up into the church, which is what I do whenever I'm there.

The church at that time of day, on a weekday, is usually empty but I saw that there was someone sitting in one of the pews, a man with his head in his hands. I instinctively drew back, not wanting to disturb him, when he lifted his head and I saw that it was Maurice Shelby. On an impulse I went up the aisle and stood beside him. He turned and saw me, looking confused and uncertain.

"Mrs. Malory—I had no idea you were here."

"I've been cleaning my husband's gravestone and I usually come in here for a while afterward. I'm sorry to have disturbed you. I hadn't realized you were a churchgoer."

"No, not usually, but I needed to—to think about something and this seemed a good place to do so."

"I believe you do have quite a lot to think about just now," I said, "and," I went on impetuously, "what more suitable place to do so than where Daniel is buried?"

He stood up suddenly. "What do you mean?"

Feeling that I'd gone too far to turn back, and knowing that Bob Morris would not approve, I said, "Because you killed him."

For a moment I thought he was going to push

past me and leave the church, but he sat down again, silent, his hands clutching the back of the pew in front of him.

"The police know about the Land Rover you hired in Bristol," I said, "and the girl there could identify you in spite of your using Martin Rogers's driving license."

He looked up at me blankly.

"And," I continued, "police forensics have found shreds of Daniel's clothing on the bumper. We know how you did it and where you parked, waiting for Dan to come by that morning. What we don't know is why."

He looked as if he was going to say something and I waited, but he remained silent.

"I imagine it was something to do with the genealogy," I said. "Patrick, Daniel's partner, has traced the line back to your connection with Eva's family—a connection you denied. Daniel was killed to stop him doing just that, wasn't he?" I paused for a moment, then I said fiercely, "If you'd known that Patrick was doing that would you have killed him too?"

"No!" The word burst from him. "No, it has all been too much. I never meant—I had no choice!" He covered his face with his hands. "Oh God, what have I done!" After a short while he said more calmly, "Perhaps this is a suitable place for a confession. Since *you* seem to know so much, please sit down and I will try to explain."

I couldn't bear to sit beside him so I sat sideways in the pew in front of him.

"There is, as you seem to know," he began, now in his usual formal manner, "a connection between our two families. My great-grandfather, William Benson, had a daughter, Martha, as well as his son James. She married a John Shelby, who was a local farmer and they had one son, my father, Arthur Shelby, who became a solicitor. I studied law because of him.

"Meanwhile James had quarreled with his father and gone away. The family had no idea where he was and he never got in touch. William Benson's wife, who had predeceased him, had been very upset at the loss of her son and he, too, came to regret the quarrel, and when he died it was found that he had left his property to be equally divided between his son and his daughter. As is customary in such cases, James was advertised for in the *London Gazette* and elsewhere, but since he had severed all links, he never came to claim his inheritance."

He paused, presumably to give me an opportunity to take in all he had said. I made no comment and he went on, "William Benson lived on into his nineties and outlived his daughter and her husband so that the inheritance came to my parents. There was a sum of money, the house and a five-acre field adjoining it, which he had purchased some years back. It was a handsome house and my parents moved into it but did nothing about the field. I believe they sold the hay to a local farmer. The house was on the edge of the village and gradually further houses were built, all substantial and expensive, and one day they were made an offer for the field by a developer. It was a very considerable sum and my father felt it would be foolish to refuse it. He used part of it to set me up in my own practice in Taunton."

"I see," I said.

"You will have seen the implications of this. After my parents died, I inherited the remaining money—a small fortune, even in those days. I took a partner, a good friend of mine, and between us we built up the practice and made it a great success. As I have said, I had always known that my grandmother had a brother, who had gone away and had never reappeared. I also checked that he had been advertised for—though, not as thoroughly as I would have wished. Then I made a mistake; I thought that after all this time there would be no one to make a claim so I omitted to take out beneficiary insurance, which would have indemnified me in the case of another claimant." He paused.

"Yes, I see," I repeated.

He nodded. "A foolish mistake. It was about this time that I became interested in genealogy. It was then that I discovered there was a line which had descended from the son who had gone away and, furthermore, that one of his descendants was actually here, living near Taviscombe. I decided to keep quiet about the connection in the hope that Eva Jackson would never find out about it. But there was some talk of her looking up her family on the Internet and I began to feel uneasy. Then, when she died, I felt safe again." I moved my head in revulsion, not being able to look at him. "You see," he continued, "I had no idea that she had a son."

He leaned forward and spoke earnestly. "I would willingly have paid back the money if that had been possible; but it was not just the sum itself, but interest on it over the years. There was no way I could have raised that sum of money. It was all gone. Not all in extravagance, though our standard of living, with the girls and so forth, was high, but I had been obliged to pay out a very large sum of money. I can tell you about it now, since the person involved is dead. I discovered that my partner, who was also my best friend, had been embezzling money from several estates of elderly clients." He paused again but I made no comment so he continued, "Fortunately, I was able to put the money back without it being discovered. My partner went abroad. I gave him a small sum of money to help him get started—as I said, he was my best friend. But then I had to run the practice on my own and, now things have changed so much in the profession, I am not able to make the sort of money that would allow me to save even a fraction of what I would owe. This discovery, about Eva Jackson and her son, would have meant they could have made a claim on the estate. I couldn't risk that. I would have been forced into bankruptcy—the shame for Alison and the girls. I had to put a stop to things and so—I did what I had to do—what I thought I had to do . . ." His voice died away and I could find nothing to say. The sound of that voice, going on and on, describing things in such a calm, matter-of-fact way, made me feel sick.

He said nothing for a moment, then he said, "I imagine you will communicate all that I have told you to the police?" I remained silent. "Naturally, you will do so." He stood up and I turned to look at him. "So," he said, "if you will excuse me, I have things to do." He inclined his head in a sort of bow, turned and went out of the church.

I don't know how long I sat there. When, eventually, I tried to get up I was very stiff from having sat so long in the hard pew. I went to the open door of the church and stood looking down at the view, trying to come to terms with what I'd heard.

Envoi

"Bob Morris gave me a very stern lecture," I said to Rosemary, "and I suppose it was foolish and dangerous, but, honestly, when I saw him there, something snapped and I couldn't help myself."

"He could have killed you!" Rosemary said. "I do wish you'd think before you plunge into things."

"I know. It was foolish," I agreed, "but I don't think he was in a state to kill anyone—he was more or less broken."

"It was still foolish," Rosemary said sternly.

"I felt so bad about not telling you what was happening, but Bob made me promise."

"That's fine. I do understand. So what has happened?"

I was silent for a moment, trying to gather my

thoughts. "When he left me," I said slowly, "he went
into his office and wrote a long and detailed confession and took it to the police station." I paused again.
"Then," I went on, "he went home, got his shotgun,
drove up onto the moor and shot himself, trying to
make it look like an accident."

"Good God."

"I know. I feel very responsible."

"That's rubbish! Of course *you* weren't to blame."

"I know that really, but I can't help feeling—well,
responsible."

"Think of Daniel."

"Yes, I do, of course I do. But it seems wrong to
sum up something so terrible just like that."

"What else is there to say?" Rosemary said. "Well,
I for one am glad he's dead and you should be too."

"Yes, I know, it is right; justice has been done and
all that—but poor Alison. I hope her daughters will
look after her."

Patrick came to see me.

"Now all this has been sorted, I'm going away,"
he said.

"Oh no! Mrs. Dudley will miss you dreadfully—
we all will!"

"I'm coming back. I like it here and I like all the
people." He gave me a rare smile. "No, I'm going
home. To Ireland. My father has died, so now I can."

I looked at him inquiringly. "Years ago," he said,
"when I 'came out' my father disowned me, threw
me out. My mother and sisters were too afraid of him

to stand up for me and my brother was too young to understand what was happening. The only person who did stand up for me was my grandmother. She was a very difficult old woman, but she was, surprisingly enough, fond of me. Mrs. Dudley reminds me of her. But even she couldn't change his mind."

"But now you can go back," I said. "I hope she's still alive."

"Oh yes. I kept in touch with her and she let me know about my father."

"That's marvelous."

"All this—seeing you all, happy and at ease with your families—even Mrs. Dudley—has made me realize how much I want my own family. Do you understand?"

"Yes I do," I said warmly, "and I'm delighted that we've helped you to feel like that. Good luck!"

And for the first, and possibly the last, time I gave him a hug.

The next night there was a violent storm. Tris, who is afraid of thunder, and Foss, who never misses an opportunity, were both on my bed. With the noise of wind and the rain outside and with the many confused thoughts running through my head, I didn't sleep well. I woke from a doze just before dawn. There was a splatter of rain against the window and I moved restlessly. Tris gave a little whine while Foss shifted to make himself more comfortable on my feet. I stretched out my hand and switched on the radio. The room was filled with a calm, steady voice:

The general synopsis at midnight. Low Faeroes 955 expected Norway 970 by midnight tonight. New low expected Rockall 984 by the same time. Forties, Cromarty, Forth, southwest veering west later 7 to severe gale 8, occasionally high in north Forties. Squally showers . . . Moderate to poor . . .

I settled back on my pillow and let the familiar words wash over me.

Also available from

Hazel Holt

MRS. MALORY AND ANY MAN'S DEATH

The village of Mere Barton would be a different
place without local busybody Annie Roberts, the
tireless retired nurse who organizes and oversees all
local activity with military precision. When Sheila
Malory gets roped into Annie's latest project, a
compilation of the village's history, she has a feeling
it will lead to trouble. But the project is cut short
when Annie is found dead from a nasty case of
mushroom poisoning and Mrs. Malory seems to be
the only one who finds the death suspicious.
Because of her nosy nature, Annie had discovered
some dark secrets about her fellow villagers—secrets
someone might kill to keep quiet.

"A wonderful heroine."
—*St. Petersburg Times*

Available wherever books are sold or at penguin.com

facebook.com/TheCrimeSceneBooks